I0651867

Isabella F. Darling

**Whispering Hope**

Isabella F. Darling

**Whispering Hope**

ISBN/EAN: 9783337085087

Printed in Europe, USA, Canada, Australia, Japan

Cover: Foto ©Andreas Hilbeck / pixelio.de

More available books at **www.hansebooks.com**

*Isa Darling*

# WHISPERING HOPE.

BY

ISABELLA F. DARLING.

EDINBURGH AND GLASGOW: JOHN MENZIES & CO.

LONDON: SIMPKIN, MARSHALL, & CO.

—

1893.

*Dundee:*
*Printed by John Leng & Co.,*
*Bank Street.*

# This Book

IS AFFECTIONATELY DEDICATED

TO MY SISTER,

## GRACE DARLING.

# CONTENTS.

8 *CONTENTS.*

# WHISPERING HOPE.

## SCOTTISH WILD FLOWERS.

O ! CHILDREN, list, the wild bells ring,
   And wave their bonnets blue ;
While heavily the lilies swing
   Their crests begemmed with dew.
Where streamlets gush 'mid ferns, and rush
   The rocks and pebbles o'er,
Come forth in bands with willing hands,
   The solitudes explore.

Come where the blue speedwell, thistle, and heather bell
Bask in the sunshine, or glance in the showers;
Buttercups sweet unfold, gowan and marigold,
Varied and beautiful, " Scottish Wild Flowers."

And think, while wandering through the glades,
   Or resting 'neath the trees,
Of buds that pine in sunless shades,
   More dear to God than these.
A child's low wail, from lips grown pale,
   Sweet eyes your aid implore :
Some little breast, by pain distressed,
   Amid the city's roar.

      Come where the blue speedwell, &c.

B

And while with eager beaming eyes
 The mountain flowers are sought,
God speeds the winner of each prize,
 And all who win it not ;
For He who knows the least of those,
 Accepts their offering free,
And whispers still by stream and hill,
 " Ye gave it unto Me."

Come where the blue speedwell, &c.

# IMITATION.

THE pulse of the world is becoming so weak,
  We will never have anything new ;
While every one waits for his neighbour to speak,
  Or to see what his neighbour will do.
And paths that we tread are so beaten and grooved,
  That little for progress is done ;
The mind of the million too often has proved
  The biassed opinion of one.

Then down with the rule that retards and enslaves,
  And the wrong that is reckoned a right ;
For fashions and customs have often been graves
  Where the soul has been buried from sight :
Where lives full of promise to chaos are hurled,
  And talents are laid on the shelf ;
But the man who is fitted to think for the world,
  Is the man who can think for himself.

Then dare to be honestly just what you are,
  And dare to be voted a crank,
For anything surely is better by far
  Than being an impotent blank.
And join in some noble, unpopular cause,
  And let your opinion be known ;
For some who are seeking the world's applause
  Will gain it by losing their own.

And give us the laughter that rings from a heart
    As warm and as bright as the sun ;
The graces of nature, unsullied by art,
    Opinions you've earnestly won.
A house built on sand shall be swiftly o'erthrown,
    The props of the wicked shall fall ;
For only the true in the end will be known
    And read and approved of by all.

# LOVE IS BLIND.

Love roved the sombre woods at noon,
Love went abroad in leafy June ;
Who said the world was out of tune ?
Who said that love was blind ?
He never viewed a brighter sky,
Its tints grew fairer to the eye ;
Nor found so many coloured flowers
In woods and crannies wild.
Oh ! brothers, what a world is ours,
With dazzling sunsets, crystal showers,
Glooms, glories, pile on pile.
God breathes through all the quivering leaves,
And o'er each dark defile,
Briar roses, where the brown bee sips,
With petals fair, like rosy lips—
Are parting with his smile.
" Ye cluster deep, ye violets sweet,
Your heads together group,
For Nature is a social king,
Who loves a royal troop."
The ferns grow up in families
Beneath the sheltering rocks ;
The young firs make the forest deep,
The lambs are all in flocks.
Love never heard so many birds
Among the tall elm trees,

Such countless throngs, nor heard such songs
Borne on the whispering breeze.
They sang till day's bright course had run,
And stars loomed overhead,
And, like a spendthrift Prince, the sun
His wealth of gold had shed.
Love lit the world, the world was blind
Till Love unveiled her eyes.
A Heaven-born glory like a mist
On earth and ocean lies—
A glory falling like a veil,
Before its light, the stars grew pale,
And Heaven was in his eyes.
But Love was blind, struck by the light
Of a maiden's eye as dark as night,
And caught in a web of tresses bright,
The glossy braids entwined
Around his strong and ample wrists,
And a small hand leads him where she lists,
For Love, sweet Love, is blind.

# WORK IT OUT.

BESIDE the fireside embers red
A father sat with drooping head.
'Twas eventide, and toil was past,
But o'er his life a shade was cast,
For he had tried, and tried in vain,
To solve the mystery of pain.
Great questions throbbing in his breast,
Despoiled him of his well-earned rest,
And as he watched the vapours rise,
With stern and meditative eyes,
Thus in his heart he sadly mused :
" God's ways are complex and confused.
Why should the strong be free from care,
And weak things get the loads to bear ?
Why say that truth will always pay ?
Here lies have often won the day.
While honours wait for churls and knaves,
Our heroes pine in dens and caves ;
In pain and want and wanderings lone,
Applauded only when they're gone.
And if our God is Love indeed,
Oft to our plaint He pays no heed ;
For hate and want and malice rude
Have often triumphed over good.
Where'er we turn, life's vital springs
Are living with these slimy things ;

Through years of direful ills we fight,
Which in a moment He could right.
How can He hear us knock and shout,
Swing His great doors and shut us out ?"
Thus wave on wave the questions rolled :
When came his boy, just six years old,
Fair-haired, with pink flushed cheeks and ears,
And dark eyes luminous with tears ;
He held his slate and pencil out,
In expectation mixed with doubt :
" Come, dear papa, and help me done,
You know the answers every one ;
Our big exam. is drawing near,
I mean to have a prize this year."
" No, Bertie, that would never do.
I work a task assigned to you !
What pleasure would it give to see
My boy with honours won by me ?
That lesson to your memory bring
Taught by the spider to a king.
Here, go, put dire despair to rout,
Be brave, my boy, and work it out."
Yes, he must teach his little son
That precious knowledge must be won ;
But swift the shaft of truth returned,
The flickering firelight brighter burned,
One trembling tear aside he dashed,
Across the doubts new meaning flashed,
For he had asked our Father, too,
To do a thing he scorned to do.

"Go work it out, go work it out—
Go strike, put dire despair to rout;
What pleasure would it give to see
My son with honours won by me?"
Thus, in a way he ne'er forgot,
He learned the lesson he had taught,
And thanked the Lord for all he knew,
And what He wisely held from view.
No more the sea of doubt o'erwhelms,
For great ships swing to little helms.

# BABY.

Two lily lids, which fall and rise
O'er dewy violets, "baby's eyes,"
Two tiny ears, like ivory shells,
Two cheeks, the bloom of heather bells,
Two lips, like buds, dew-kissed and wet,
Two teeth ! like pearls, in pink are set.
Two dimpled arms, a hand with each,
Pale pink, and waxen like the peach,
Two rosy, restless little feet,
Make baby's double charms complete.

One little face of finest mould,
One lovely head of downy gold,
One cry which wakens answering thrills,
And ev'ry little want fulfils,
One spotless heart, one mind he bears,
One joy, he makes a thousand cares,
One constant care, an endless joy,
One angel, like a baby boy,
One gift, comprising every grace,
One little bunch of lawn and lace.

Oh ! ye whose heads have hoary grown,
In searching for the Great Unknown,
While here to earth the cherub brings
So much of Heaven on his wings.

What love unspoken lights his eyes—
This weak thing still confounds the wise.
This poem, bud of life, unblown,
The language of the lines unknown,
Life's mystic journey scarce begun ;
A race that never shall be run,
A picture in an earthly frame,
Where all must read the author's name.

# A BIRTHDAY WISH.

WHAT shall I wish thee, my bonnie boy?
    Said his grandsire, aged and grey ;
I wish thee health, I wish thee joy,
    Since this is thy natal day.
Though I know full well that the golden spell
    Of childhood's morn will break ;
When storm and cloud, the blue enshroud,
    And the hills with thunder quake,
    The dreamer to life must awake.

What shall I wish thee, my little lad,
    My boy with the shining eye?
I wish thee always gay and glad,
    With never a cloudy sky ;
Yet well I know, and 'tis better so,
    The lightest heart must mourn.
The bright stars sleep, the sad hours creep,
    And the fires of anguish burn,
    Ere thy gold locks to silver turn.

But romp, my lad, be blythe and gay,
    You came with the opening flowers ;
You came to-day, with your mirth and play,
    To this grand old world of ours.
I, who have stood through its mortal feud,
    Have reaped for wrong redress ;

With my laurels won, from duty done,
   And I cannot wish thee less
   Than to fight well where brave hearts press.

Not less than these, not a life of ease,
   But rest from the toil of years ;
A song that wakes, though the bosom aches,
   And smiles that break from tears.
And be thine to win from the strife within,
   Peace death shall ne'er destroy ;
The victor's shout that rings o'er doubt,
   And the crown of exceeding joy,
   These all be thine, my bonnie boy.

## THE REAL AND THE TRUE.

THE fleecy clouds are lifting fast,
   Like snowwreaths to the blue ;
Through dreamland we are drifting to
   The real and the true.
The pleasures here we count so dear,
   The duties we pursue,
Are shadows of the coming days—
   The real and the true.

Though here are true hearts seeming false,
   And cold hearts seeming kind ;
Some maxims famed of wisdom void,
   And beauty wanting mind :
Here artificial blossoms glow
   With nature's pearly dew,
And fickle, false affection, like
   The real and the true ;

Remember ! when the heart is sad,
   And tears begem the cheek,
That just behind the shadow lies
   The substance that we seek.
Through gain and loss, from Crown and Cross,
   The soul demands its due,
And nothing will suffice us but
   The real and the true.

Let courage meet with dire defeat,
  Be heroes strong and bold ;
For in the fiery furnace heat
  God tries the precious gold.
And hold them fast who brave the blast—
  The steadfast, faithful few ;
For priceless in the battle are
  The real and the true.

Earth's tawdry treasures turn to dust,
  Her triumphs turn to shame ;
The seed will be the flower soon,
  The spark will be the flame ;
The weak will throng to quell the strong,
  To conquer and subdue ;
For victory is the birthright of
  The real and the true.

## "THE GREATEST."

WHEN soft winds sighed through the leafy boughs,
  And birds were a' in tune,
The Maister cam' frae the dark-green knowes,
  Into the steer 'o' the toun.

And fisher lads left their boats in the bay
  To the billows' heave and swell,
For the Lord had wunnerfu' thochts that day,
  And wunnerfu' things to tell.

The young were there, and the rich and puir,
  And some wi' aches and pains,
White heads bowed down wi' time and care,
  And bonnie, winsome weans.

When He carried oor care in His silvered hair,
  Oor shame on His youthfu' broo,
Muckle He thocht o' the lost that He socht,
  But spakena: His heart was fu'.

Angry and loud are the words that fa'
  Sae harshly on His ear:
"Wha'll be the greatest among us a'?"
  Quo' Peter, "Let us speer!"

And the stalwart fishermen drew near,
  Wi' meikle speed to learn;

They thocht the Maister didna hear,
    For He cried inower a bairn.


Wi' locks blawn free, and gled, bricht e'e,
    The couthie wee thing ran ;
Quo' the Maister, " Let him ower to Me,
    Stan' yont here ! My wee man."


And He patted the bairnie's chubby cheek,
    As red as the bonnie haw—
And He said, " I wadna gae far to seek
    The greatest among ye a'.


The wisest o' the warld maun learn
    That he wha comes to Me
'Maun be as trustfu' as a bairn,
    In spirit jist as wee.


The king, and the saint, and the sage will meet
    At the yett o' my Faither's Ha',
But the bairnie wi' his toddlin' feet
    Gangs in afore them a'."


They gethered roond in sair amaze,
    And glowered to hear sic lore ;
For oh ! they ne'er in a' their days
    Had heard sic words afore.


Little they kent o' the Gospel plan,
    And little they understood

c

The kingly heart o' that weary Man,
   Sae lonely 'mang the crood.

He was puir and lane, when He cam' to His ain,
   Gaun hameless on the street ;
But the wark He has done is the glory aboon,
   And the world is at His feet.

# LOVE UNEXPRESSED.

'Tis not enough that I should know,
  I cannot understand,
A love that brooks no overflow,
  No pressure of the hand.
You say the heart within is warm,
  Is true and good as gold ;
I only see the outward form,
  So tranquil and so cold.

'Tis not enough that I should know ;
  If 'mid the strife and din,
I miss the tender deeds which show
  That love still lives within.
The sun breaks forth through cloudy rifts,
  From darkness brighter glows ;
And love is lavish with her gifts,
  Nor weight nor measure knows.

'Tis not enough, when joy-beams shine,
  To join me in my mirth,
If seldom here when joys decline
  You seek the mourner's hearth.
'Tis not enough to say " You feel,"
  When sorrows overpower,
If never from the crowd you steal
  To weep with me one hour.

'Tis not enough, with chilling gaze,
  To say you chide for love ;
If never 'once, in friendly praise,
  Your eyes or lips approve.
Then wait not with your words of cheer
  Till Death's dew chills the brow,
For then they will not care to hear,
  Who yearn and hunger now.

If Love still lives, withhold it not ;
  The Love each spirit pleads
Must sometimes blossom forth from thoughts,
  And show itself in deeds.
" Love unexpressed !" a starless gloom,
  A dead sea—mute and lone ;
A soul within a living tomb ;
  A sun that never shone.

Then loose the floodgates, throw them wide !
  The heart's true light reveal ;
Nor longer 'neath the crust of pride
  Your better self conceal ;
Lest o'er your bliss a shade be cast,
  When heaven's goal is won,
For flowers that braved the wintry blast,
  And died without the sun.

## "NOTHING TO DO."

OH, ye who pity the humble poor,
  Let a silent tear-drop fall
For the direful ills that hearts endure
  Who haven't a care at all—
Who haven't a tear to shed.
  For sorrowing ones below—
    Not a joy to share, nor a smile to spare,
  In a world o'erwhelmed with woe.

      Nothing, nothing to learn,
        For everything he knows,
      Nothing to prove, and nothing to love,
        And reaping what he sows ; ·
      No drooping hearts to cheer,
        No calling to pursue,
      How can he live with nothing to give,
        And nothing, nothing to do ?

The pure, sweet gowans that deck the green,
  Peep out when they see him pass,
And nod behind their grassy screen,
  And whisper, " Alas ! alas !"
" We've all got a song to sing !"
  Trills the lark from the vaulted blue,
And the river weeps, as it glides and sweeps,
  For the man who finds nothing to do.

      Nothing, nothing to learn, &c.

His carriage may roll in princely state,
　　But he hasn't a princely mind ;
The world may count him rich and great,
　　But he's wretched, poor, and blind.
With his life yet scarce begun,
　　And endless years in view,
Save in the tomb, there is found no room
For a man who finds nothing to do.

Nothing, nothing to learn, &c.

# ONE IN ALL.

A THOUSAND leaves, of varying shade,
  Are trembling on one tree,
A thousand streams, from wooded glades,
  Are hastening to one sea ;
Ten thousand flowers, in wood and glen,
  Are turning to the sun ;
And all the varied minds of men
  Derive their light from One.

Thus, where we roam we seek one home—
  One hope each soul sustains ;
One light shall gild the Jordan's foam—
  One rest for all remains.
For man may meet, and man may part,
  In search of Truth and Light ;
But as he thinketh in his heart,
  So is he wrong or right.

Yet He who rides and rules the storm,
  Man's wisdom laughs to scorn ;
Who casts a thousand tints to form
  The glory of one morn ;
Whose mercies ever round us fall,
  While He, in countless ways,
Draws joy and harmony from all—
  From discord perfect praise.

# OOR AIN.

Oh, sing na to me o' yer lands far awa',
    Or skies that are foreign and fair ;
Yer hills and yer howes, were they ever sae braw,
    Wi' Scotland's they winna compare.
Its lads are the bravest, its lassies the brawest,
    For valour it stan's by its lane ;
            Gang east or gang west,
            It's the land we like best ;
Oh, there's nane wad compare wi' oor ain,
Let us own't, and be fair wi' oor ain.

And if we should dwell in a fine marble ha',
    And walk on a saft velvet pile,
Hoo often oor thochts will tak' wing, and awa'
    To a hame in oor ain native isle ;
And the heart hoo it fills, tho' 'twere auld as the hills,
    That wee cot, auldfashioned and plain,
            Ay, we craw aye fu' crouse
            In oor ain cantie hoose,
For the brawest and blithest's oor ain ;
Bless the hoosie ! there's nane like oor ain.

And if 'mang oorsel's we hae sometimes a tift,
    And differ and cangle awee,
It's jist like a cloud passin' ower the blue lift ;
    We quarrel, but we're sure aye to gree.

Sae dinna let on, till the bicker blaws by ;
    For, mind ye, we're friends in the main.
        Then whatever betide,
        Dinna tak' ony side,
Or we'll say the concern is oor ain,
For we'll gree yet, and haud by oor ain.


To think sic a halo o' pleasure should fa'
    Roond oorsel's, and oor gifts, and oor gear,
While the interests o' ithers are flung to the wa',
    It's this that mak's misery here ;
But the wisest soon see they maun tak' what they gie,
    Whiles it's hard, but they canna complain,
        But the king among men,
        And there's ane among ten,
Can feel for a grief no his ain,
And be gled though the gain's no his ain.


Respect aye a man wi' a mind o' his ain,
    Though his way is no your way ava ;
If you canna gang wi' him, just gang by your lane,
    There is room in the warld for a'.
And if we're no happy and hearty the noo,
    When time wi' its troubles has gane,
We maybe will see, when the beam's oot our e'e,
    Hoo muckle the faut was oor ain,
    And we'll own it the faut was oor ain.

## THE AULD THORN TREE.

" Come, lassies, here an' rest awee,"
　　Quo' Annie o' the Ha',
" A simmer day's aye best to me,
　　Just in the gloamin' fa'.
I'm shure it's fifty years an' mair
　　Sin' I was young an' spree,
Gaun scamperin' wi' my cronies
　　Round this auld thorn tree.

Hoo often in an afternoon,
　　Aneath the tree we'd meet ;
The clear blue lift high up aboon,
　　The gowans at oor feet.
My faither read, my mither sewed,
　　Or watched wi' kindly e'e
Oor capers an' oor cantrips,
　　'Neath the auld thorn tree.

Here, too, at nicht-fa, frae the Lynn,
　　Cam' Donald wi' his plaid,
To meet me when the bonnie moon
　　Keeked through the branches braid.
Then, steppin' quate, I slippet oot—
　　For aye his tryst wi' me,
Was, ' Annie, I'll be waitin'
　　At the auld thorn tree.'

Noo years fa' white on ilka heid,
    Braw locks to silver turn,
And lassies' cheeks, like roses red
    On briers by the burn,
Hae lang syne tint their bonnie bloom,
    But aye they're fair to me,
When sittin' wi' my knittin',
    'Neath the auld thorn tree.

Though here oor pleasures bloom to fa',
    An' kind friends meet to part,
Wi' cauldrife care my heid's like snaw,
    But simmer's in my heart ;
The dear anes lost I'll meet again,
    Whaur leal heart's love will be
Even purer than the blossom
    On the auld thorn tree."

## "THE UNDESERVING POOR."

DWELLERS in the crowded city,
   Where the haunts of vice allure,
Have you felt no human pity
   For the undeserving poor ?

Lives embittered, eyes appealing,
   Lost souls meet us everywhere ;
Their's the wound without the healing,
   Their's the pain without the prayer.

Saints, philosophers, and sages
   Say, " Their doom is well deserved,
Let them reap their ghastly wages,
   From the master they have served."

Backward on their wrongs they're driven,
   " Well deserved " their deepest woe ;
This the pang unknown to heaven,
   This the saddest blight below.

Chide not, turn not from their weeping,
   Who have found for wrong redress ;
If they merit what they're reaping,
   Will it make the suffering less ?

When you turn them from your portals,
   Scorned as souls by Satan bound,

One who died for erring mortals,
　Stoops, and writes upon the ground.

One alone among the living,
　Who is holy, good, and pure,
Left the righteous unforgiving
　For the undeserving poor.

Leave the bitter thought unspoken,
　Since thou can'st not throw the stone;
To the Heart for sinners broken,
　Leave them with their Lord alone.

# LINES ON THE BAPTISM OF THE LADY ALEXANDRA DUFF.

WHEN summer's bright blossoms bespangled the green,
And the red rose was breaking her heart to be queen ;
When wild crimson bells set the heather aflame,
A fair little flower from the mountain land came—
   A sweet little baby,
   Petite little baby,
A lady of title and fame.


'Mid blazing of diamonds and glitter of gold,
That little Scotch lady was fair to behold,
Her downy robe falling in soft pearly showers;
She recked not of princes, or sceptres, or powers,
   But raised a clear treble—
   The dear little rebel—
Babies have language as well as the flowers.


The crystals from Jordan were brightly aglow
On that little pink bud in a garden of snow,
When acting on impulse she could not resist,
She dropt her silk lashes and clenched her small fist.
   Oh ! 'twas right royal sport,
   Her contempt of the Court,
When the dew-begemmed rosebud was kissed.

The Queen of the land came to soothe her alarms,
And folded her close in her motherly arms;
And though but an infant, the babe was impressed
That 'twas good to recline on a motherly breast—
  And she closed each soft lid
  Till the bright eyes were hid,
Like a wee downy bird in its nest.


Saith the rose, bending meek from a green, mossy bough,
" I will twine a bright wreath for the fair dreamer's brow;"
" We lilies are sweet," sighed a voice from the bowers,
" But not half so pure as this Princess of ours."
  " She is fairer than we !"
  Sighed the flowers on the lea ;
" We'll crown her the queen of the flowers !"
  .  .  .  .  .  .

May Heaven's best blessings illumine thy home,
And keep thee as pure as the dazzling sea foam,
And give thee, when time's ebbing billows recede,
A name that is honoured by mountain and mead ;
  The Scots of our island,
  Both Lowland and Highland,
Enjoin me to wish thee God-speed !

## "ALL IS WELL."

"God is in Heaven—all's well,"
Heaven, oh, where does its pure mansions rise?
Tearful we gaze on the fathomless skies:
"Lies round our infancy," poets have sung;
Dawns with the soul when its morning is young.
Where can we search for it, how can we find,
If daily our Heaven we're leaving behind?
Is innocence Heaven?—better to stand
Fighting the battle of life, hand-to-hand,
Steadfast and pure while the vile tempests brood—
Knowing the evil, yet choosing the good;
Surely to such has the watchword been given,
" All is well with the earth—God is in heaven."

Say, is it well with the earth?
Nature responsive thy misery grieves;
Wounded, dejected, and fallen 'mong thieves;
Helpless and bleeding and fainting you lie,
White clouds above you, like Levites pass by;
Yet, it is well, there is sweet gain in woe,
Blessings that only the sorrowful know,
Life, deathless life, in thy frail, fleeting breath,
Love, 'mid the ruins wild, laughing at Death:
Gem, all begrimed with the dust of the mine,
"One lost," for whom was left ninety-and-nine,
Still to thy Maker unspeakably dear;
Heaven sounds far away.  Courage!  God's here.

"God's in His world, all is well,"
Sang by a bird as he flew through the wood
Searching for food for his dear downy brood ;
Taught by a flower in a green valley lone,
Flashed from a sunbeam, and read in a stone,
Babbled by pure baby brooks as they pass,
Uttered in thunder's loud sonorous bass,
Printed on snow-clouds in fire letters bold.
Painted at daybreak in silver and gold.
Say not He dwells in some far distant sphere,
Beat through the silence His heart-throbs we hear,
Starred nightly o'er us, His banners unfurled,
"All is well with the earth, God's in His world."

"God's in His world, all is well,"
Here, where the fools mock, and say He is not,
Here where His glorious battles are fought,
Here where the river of Death must be crossed,
Just where we need Him, and call for Him most ;
Back from the field with an infinite gain,
Victory from failure, and triumph from pain,
Greet the all-conquering King with a cheer,
Doubt not His presence, His treasure is here ;
Life's grand Creator knows best how to live,
Crown of His glory, the weak to forgive ;
Ring joyous bells while " the best robe" is given—
"All is well " with the earth, God is in Heaven.

# SUNDERED.

SHE will never come to me
In the spring, when boughs are wreathing,
Perfume from the milk thorn breathing,
Tulip, crocus, snowdrop dewy,
Blue and crimson, gold and pearly,
  Fresh and early;
With her mirth the echoes waking,
Thought on thought impetuous breaking
Like the wavelets of the sea;
Never shall I hear her calling,
Never hear her light foot falling—
She will never come to me.

She will never come to me
When the sparkling shower passes;
Daisies star the emerald grasses,
Flower bells from the meadow ringing,
Damask buds, with petals parted,
  Sunny-hearted;
When the spreading fruit tree flowereth
And the fair laburnum showereth
Yellow tresses o'er the lea;
When the downy bee is humming
I will never wait her coming—
She will never come to me.

She will never come to me
When the autumn leaf is drooping,
And the golden sheaf is stooping,
Dark-eyed poppies, waving scarlet,
Through the stubble, speeding, slowing,
      Cheeks aglowing;
Where the brambles trail and clamber,
Brown leaves, tinted rose and amber,
Jetty fruited, wild and free,
Saddest thought, with tears o'erflowing,
With the seasons coming, going—
She will never come to me.

She will never come to me,
In the snow time, never! never!
When the cold flakes whirl and shiver,
Floating, falling, drifting, fleeting,
Never by the firelight cosy,
      Bright and rosy;
Never singing in the twilight,
Blue eyes deepening into violet,
Laughter loving, fair to see.
Holly boughs and berries glisten,
And the years come back to listen—
But she cannot come to me.

She will never come to me.
I will go, when life is over,
Where no gloomy shadows hover,
'Mongst the living I will meet her,

Where earth's blossoms, frail and sickly,
    Freshen quickly ;
She is safe in God's own keeping,
To the toiling and the weeping
I will never call her more ;
Let her slumber till she waketh,
He who giveth most, and taketh,
Always keeps the best in store.

# RESCUE WORK.

A LURID glare in the dusky sky,
   A cry at midnight hour;
Now, like bounding hail the bright sparks fly,
   A burning, golden shower.
The clouds are tinged with a fiery fringe
   Behind the tall church spire,
The tumult breaks and the city wakes—
   Fire! Fire! Fire!

      Clear the way for the Fire Brigade!
      They cannot brook delay,
      When driving past, like the roaring blast,
      To the fierce and fiery fray;
      In the scorching breath
      Of the phantom Death,
      Undaunted, undismayed;
      When the strong have failed,
      And the bravest paled—
      Clear the way for the Fire Brigade!

'Tis life or death, to the rescue fly!
   Fire! fire! awake! awake!
From the weary brow and dreamy eye
   The dews of slumber shake!

A face gleams white on the giddy height,
  O Father, shield the brave !
'Mid piercing cries, through the smoke they rise,
  Help ! help !—save !

    Clear the way for the Fire Brigade, &c.


The conqueror comes with the roll of drums,
  While martial banners flow;
Unsung, unknown, 'mid the crowd, alone,
  Our heroes come and go.
Then cheer below, while they quell the foe ;
  Let it ring through the midnight clear,
When the weak are saved, and the danger braved,
  Cheer ! cheer ! cheer !

    Clear the way for the Fire Brigade, &c.

## "SONG OF THE CLYDE."

I COME from haunts of heather bells,
  The home of brave and mighty men ;
With native pride my bosom swells,
  As I rush through the fir-clad glen
To "rock the cradle of the deep"
  On the billow's crest of foam ;
To sport with the winds, when the tempests sweep,
  With joy I roam to seek my home.

      For the voice of ocean breaks my rest
        With a song so wild and free,
      That I sing, as I roll to the glowing west,
        The sea for me—the grand lone sea.


'Neath shady ferns the silver trout
  Dart from the rocks and disappear,
When prying sunbeams call me out
  My laughter ripples soft and clear ;
And lashed to foam, my current brown
  Awakens the woods from sleep,
And the rugged hills look so grandly down
  To see me leap from Cora's steep.

      For the voice of ocean, &c.


Soon, deep and still, my dark tide gleams
  'Neath old St Mungo's arches strong ;

I reach the city with the streams
    That have joined me gliding along.
The tall masts quiver when I call,
    Like leaves on an aspen tree ;
On my heaving breast they shall rise and fall,
    And seek with me the grand old sea.

    For the voice of ocean, &c.

## " THE DAY WE NEVER SAW."

THE warld's gaun dune afore us a',
  Fast speeds this waefu' day,
Will nae bit sunny glint ava'
  Be shining through the grey?
Gae coont the cost o' time that's lost
  Among us ane an' a',
Despairing and preparing
  For " the day we never saw."

    It's " the day we never saw,"
    And the clouds that never fa',
    And the weary care that's coming,
    That we canna bear ava';
    Bonnie een are dim wi' tears,
    And heads are white as snaw,
    Wi' thinkin' o' " the day we never saw."

In bygone days, when sorrow's haze
  O'ershadowed a' the blue,
We, like the sun, through darksome days,
  Hae bravely wars'led through.
Sae, e'en we'll find they're silver-lined,
  The clouds that never fa',
That's lowering, aye, and show'ring,
  Owre " the day we never saw."

    It's " the day we never saw," &c.

Let blithesome hope oor cares dispel,
 And dry the waefu' tear ;
We dinna ken, we canna tell,
 What human hearts can bear ;
When ills betide, we hae a Guide
 Wi' heart aboon them a',
Aye cheering, never fearing
 " For " the day we never saw."

  It's " the day we never saw," &c.

# WALLACE THE BRAVE.

CROWNS have been shattered which monarchs have cherished,
  Songs have been hushed in the banqueting hall,
Kingdoms have fallen, and heroes have perished,
  Time like an ocean sweeps over them all.
Still on the roll of fame, Scotia's proudest name
  Lives in the land that he perished to save;
Wallace, the friend of right; Wallace, the peerless knight—
  King of the Lionhearts, Wallace the Brave.

    Still is thy name revered,
    Still to our hearts endeared,
      Dread to the tyrant, and hope to the slave;
    Bright from the gloom of years,
    Gemmed by a nation's tears,
      King of the Lionhearts, Wallace the Brave.


Daughters of Scotland, the star flower uncloses,
  Gather fair blossoms, and twine him a wreath;
Snowbells and ivy, and white dewy roses,
  Sweet drooping lilies, and rare pearly heath.
Wallace was brave for thee, scorning the grave for thee;
  Exiled and hunted by mountain and cave,
'Mid the wild pibroch's wail, crown him with blossoms pale,
  King of the Lionhearts, Wallace the Brave.

    Still is thy name revered, &c.

Still from the sentinel mountains thou'rt keeping
   Vigils of love o'er thy heathery plain,
Crowned with the stars, while the millions are reaping
   Peace from thy conflict, and bliss from thy pain.
Land of the brave and free, what may we dream of thee,
   While the long billows lament round his grave ;
Broad may thy thistle grow, proud may thy banner flow,
   Home of the Lionheart, Wallace the Brave.

     Still is thy name revered, &c.

# BETHLEHEM'S STAR.

OH! EARTH, thou art seeking a King! we have found Him,
 The Monarch of all :
The sage and the shepherd were kneeling around Him
 In Bethlehem's stall.
Awake! for the eve of a great visitation
 Hath shadowed the sky;
The heavens were stilling in deep expectation
 To hear a child cry.

With harp and with song the angels alighted
 In glad shining throngs
To gaze on His face, ere its beauty was blighted
 With sufferings and wrongs,
Proclaiming to earth that a Saviour was given,
 This bright Christmas Eve;
The hope of the world, and the glory of Heaven,
 Adore and believe.

Oh, would thou had'st known in the darkness arising,
 The Sun of thy peace;
The rapture of blessing, the love realising,
 That gives to increase.
The balm for thy wounds and thy solace in sorrow,
 Hopes dawning from fears;
The deep spring of pleasures unending that borrow
 Their lustre from tears.

With glad hearts and voices, oh ! hasten to hail Him
      With timbrel and song ;
Thy King, though the cloud of humanity veil Him,
      Thy conqueror strong ;
The hand that shall wrestle your land from the stranger,
      So fragile and weak ;
In frailty behold Him, " a babe in a manger,"
      " The Lord whom ye seek."

# GOD'S BOUNTY.

God spake, but language was inadequate
To give expression to His mighty heart ;
Methinks, when silence fell, His thoughts leapt forth
In myriad stars, athwart the vast blue dome ;
His spirit, rushing with the limpid waves,
Sang love's undying symphonies,
Broke ceaselessly, beat tirelessly upon a thousand shores.
With bounteous hand He fringed the rugged hills with
      furze and pine,
The mountain ash, the silver fir, the beech,
The fruit trees with their freighted arms flung out,
The bramble vines, weighed down 'mid grasses tall,
Peep forth with jetty eyes, stretch laden hands,
Yet leave Him half revealed.
How much He loves ! the flowers breathe and are silent,
The corn stalks droop their golden heads abashed,
To show so little ;
The rivers sweep their glassy floods along, deep murmuring ;
The mountain voices utter, and are dumb.
Oh ! doubting heart of man, so deaf
When nature pours her grand thanksgiving,
Soft cradled in the lap of luxuries,
And curtained o'er with heaven :
'Tis love that radiates the eye of night,

The evening's sweet, appealing, yearning light.
Bow down where language failed.
In God's own temple let His peace steal down,
Like dew refreshing, sink within thy soul :
Here royal silence reigneth, crowned with gold,
And Love is Love that never can be told.

# CUPID.

MAY laughed at Love, and lived in truth,
　Oblivious of his sway ;
Until she met a roving youth
　Upon a happy day.

Through summer's dream-clouds fiery red,
　Eve shot a golden gleam ;
And down the rocky cliff there sped
　A foamy, leaping stream.

Love's laughter filled the leafy shade,
　He flapped his wings with glee ;
Quoth he, " I'll teach this lily maid
　To jest and laugh at me."

And forth his fairy bow he drew,
　And soon the deed was done ;
" One arrow's quite enough for two,
　When two will soon be one."

Love frowned, the world grew dark as night,
　May droopt her pretty head
Like flower in winter's early blight ;
　" Oh ! cruel Love," she said.

Love smiled, the fairy flowerets weaved
    Their garlands 'neath her feet ;
The ocean's breast with laughter heaved,
    " Oh ! Love," she sighed, " how sweet !'

Now Love, her crown that never fades,
    Is prized all gifts above ;
She whispers to the merry maids,
    " Oh ! do not laugh at Love !"

So swift is he, you cannot see
    He bears a bow and quiver ;
I laughed at Love, and now at me
    The rogue is laughing ever.

## NO CROSS, NO CROWN.

I WISHED thee joy, and lo, a plaintive strain
   Re-echoed through the silence of my heart ;
   I saw the curtain of the future part ;
My thought, unwitting, touched a mystic chain,
Connecting grief with joy, and loss with gain.

" Bright be thy path," I cried, " with roses gay ;"
   But 'neath their scented petals lurks the thorn,
   And hands that pluck them from their boughs are torn ;
Yea, feet must bleed along the heavenward way,
And those who conquer first must brave the fray.

Life's purest pleasure, like the snowdrop, wakes
   Not in the gold of summer's slanting floods,
   Where varied flowerets ope their clustering buds ;
Lo, dauntless through the cold dark earth it breaks,
Decked from the blast by winter's pearly flakes.

The rose is cased in thorns, our hopes in fears ;
   Day spreads her golden pinions o'er the night ;
   Beyond the valley looms the mountain height ;
Chaste after storms the lily's stalk uprears,
Most beautiful beneath its cup of tears.

Thus highest bliss with deepest grief is fraught.
　Be thine the light that radiates the eyes
　Of one who strives and dares to win the prize—
The joy that springs when treasures dearly bought
Roll inland on the billows of deep thought.

Joy springs from sorrow.　He who loveth best,
　Who stooped to wear for us a thorny crown,
　For joy before Him set, His life laid down ;
Who, conquering death, restored to life its zest,
And dying gave the weary endless rest.

## THE MONARCH IS THE MIND.

Y<small>E</small> merry Lords of Labour,
   Our nation's Pride and Power,
Come, hail! with hearty ringing cheers,
   The heroes of the hour;
Your thousand, thousand hands fulfil
   A task by one assigned;
Proclaiming, with a Royal will,
   The monarch is the mind.
Let Genius claim her homage still—
   The monarch is the mind.

Their works proclaim them mighty,
   Their thunders shake the world,
While streaming vapours to the sky
   In cloudy wreaths are curled;
Like giant ship that sportive plays
   With death, in wave and wind,
The will has found a thousand ways
   Untraversed, unconfined;
Their works bespeak them highest praise—
   The monarch is the mind.

Then forward, mighty monarch,
   Though threatening tempests lower,
The viewless solitudes of thought
   With fearless eye explore.

Go ! tune the harp of thousand strings
　To melodies refined,
And tireless mount on Hope's glad wings
　O'er want and death combined :
From dire defeat your triumph springs—
　The monarch is the mind.

Shine, golden star of genius,
　Thy beams impartial fall
Above the peasant's lowly cot
　And o'er the princely hall.
Where'er you stand in silent state,
　The waking world shall find,
Amid her kings and courtiers great,
　The monarch is the mind ;
The hands upon the head must wait—
　The monarch is the mind.

# KING SELF.

THIS monarch reigns with an iron hand,
   They're fools who seek to please him;
Give! give! is his royal command,
But neither the wealth of sea or land
   Was ever known to appease him.

Full, broad, and wide his empire lies,
   Vast as the heavens above it;
He might and right and truth defies,
And day and night his greedy eyes
   See nought they do not covet.

Earth knelt down to that tyrant bold
   In meek and rapt devotion,
She crowned him with a tire of gold,
And she gave him riches and wealth untold,
   And pearls from the depths of the ocean.

He holds her but a captive slave,
   Bound by a golden fetter,
He took her gifts, and nothing gave;
But give! give! said the grasping knave,
   And he sighed for something better.

## KING SELF.

The sun glows warm, the rain descends,
    Spring showers her branches o'er him,
While lavish Nature takes and spends,
His selfishness frustrates his ends,
    And pleasure flies before him.

Each victory that he gains reveals
    Hope routed, wisdom flying;
Amongst the strong his blows he deals,
And cruelly his chariot wheels
    Crush down the dead and dying.

Go, break his sceptre, spurn his laws,
    They find themselves who lose him;
And fight in freedom's holy cause,
And gain their heart's sincere applause
    Who cross and crush and bruise him.

With Death he drives his iron car,
    And shows no human pity;
Go! give him battle, scar for scar,
Who conquers him is greater far
    Than he who takes a city.

## A DAY.

Look not lightly on a day,
  Which thy God hath given :
Slight not, in thy little way,
  Aught that comes from Heaven.

Messenger of love to all,
  With its winds caressing,
Shafts of light, which break and fall,
  Like our Father's blessing.

Field and meadow, flower and tree,
  Joyous, hail its coming :
Laden, like a golden bee
  On its journey humming.

Wouldst thou, o'er the shining track,
  To the Lord who liveth,
Shed one ray of lustre back
  Of the light He giveth ?

Take the blessing that it brings
  With a thankful spirit ;
Scorn not thou the little things
  Which thou canst not merit.

## A DAY.

Leave to-morrow's care and task
  To a wise Creator,
Surely He the least may ask
  Who has borne the greater.

As thou sowest thou shalt reap;
  Night's dark curtain falleth;
But the day that sinks to sleep
  Ever wakeful calleth.

Days are standing at thy gate,
  Crowns of Joy and Sorrow;
Bright-eyed sentinels that wait
  For the long to-morrow.

## SUMMER'S AWA'.

Nae mair in the bleak woods the mavis is singin',
 The swallow is wingin' his flight o'er the main,
Ilk' flower in the garden its wee heid is hingin',
 Or lying fu' laich 'mang the stour and the rain.
And tearfu' and tender the sun's farewell glimmer
 Lights gowden and saft on the leaves as they fa':
The dark waves are soundin' a dirge for the summer,
 And mournin' fu' eerily, "Summer's awa'."

Noo lanesome the burnie gangs croonin' and jowin',
 The summer's awa', wi' its branches sae green;
The shades are deserted where lovers were vowin',
 And bairnies were daffin' and wadin' at e'en.
Ower black hills the rain clouds are driftin' and trailin',
 Wi' lang wreaths o' vapour as white as the snaw;
Through drookit trees leafless the sad winds are wailin',
 They sich aye, and sab aye, the summer's awa'.

Then bright let the licht o' the ingle be blazin,'
 While cauld raindraps rattle and drip frae the pane;
Spring, summer, and autumn are welcome in season,
 For ilk' has a beauty and joy o' its ain.
And while to the far south the summer is flying,
 Some sad hearts await ye in cottage and ha',
And some far ahint ye, ance droopin' an' dyin',
 Are licht noo and bricht noo though summer's awa'.

# THE REASON WHY.

As many flowers in summer bloom,
  As branch and meadow laden,
As many varied moods I own,
  Live in one perfect maiden ;
Yet, such is my affection,
I could not make selection,
  Since I've confessed that each is best—
Becoming, to perfection.

And as a sailor scans the skies,
  Forecasting wind and weather,
The language of her lovely eyes
  I read and put together.
When critical, I fear her ;
Contrary, I revere her ;
  Her failings all, both great and small,
Seem only to endear her.

Yet were sweet Minnie's winsome face
  Ne'er touched with shade of frowning,
Ah, where were then the rapt embrace
  Our little conflicts crowning ?
How fair my Queen appears
When shadows, doubts, and fears,
  Like frost and snow, in love's warm glow,
Dissolve in April tears.

And since her eyes are deeply blue,
  I love the pansy blossom ;
Since cheeks have tint, the rose's hue,
  I'll pluck it for her bosom.
For daily I discover
Her caprices improve her ;
  New beauties rise, and in them lies
The reason why I love her.

## "SOME BONNIE DAY."

"Some bonnie day, when the bright sun is shining,"
  Sang a fond mother her baby to sleep,
Gold-burnishèd locks on her bosom reclining,
  Dreamy eyes watching the fire dance and leap.
      "Hush thee, my little one,
      Out in the golden sun,
      Tiny wee feet will run—
        Some bonnie day."

Mother is dreaming, while night shades are creeping—
  Dreaming of shadows that darken the years;
Feet will grow weary of running and leaping,
  High hopes will blossom and vanish in tears.
      Pale sorrow waits for all,
      Duty's stern battle-call
      Wakes him to rise or fall—
        Some bonnie day.

Mother is praying that sin, care, and sadness
  Blight not the flower folded close to her breast;
Heaven, the fountain and crown of her gladness,
  Grant all her wishes, the dearest and best;
      Joy from the light that lies
      In baby's dreaming eyes,
      O'er her life's evening rise—
        Some bonnie day.

# TO A FLIRT.

Like pale rose leaves in blossom,
   These eyelids, fringed with gold ;
Thy face and pearly bosom
   Like marble pure and cold ;
Thine eyes like violets dewy,
   So sweetly, deeply blue—
Oh ! would that they were true, lady,
   Would that they were true.

The curls that round thee cluster
   Are gold in every ring,
But beauty's glowing lustre
   Shall fade like flowers of spring ;
And since on fleeting beauty
   Thou sett'st unbounded store,
Thou'lt learn that love is more, lady—
   Love and truth are more.

For, oh ! 'tis pastime cruel
   For such a soft-eyed dove
With smiles to add the fuel,
   And make a jest of love ;
With all thy charms alluring,
   'Tis nature's highest art
To feign thou hast a heart, lady—
   Heaven's royal gift, a heart.

## BEGONE, DULL REPINING.

Oh ! why should a young life in sighing be spent ?
   One shadow obscuring the lustre of morn ;
And why should a maiden a lover lament
   Whose fickle affection but merits her scorn ?
Begone ! dull repining, the night's shade discloses
   A thousand bright stars in the firmament grand ;
Be off with your lilies, and on with your roses,
   " The time of the singing of birds is at hand."
     Begone, dull repining, hope's spring-time renew,
     Light born of the darkness is breaking for you ;
     A love without reason can never be true,
     And surely 'twere treason to marry and rue.

Gaze not on the clouds that above you impend,
   Beyond them the blue sky beams soft and serene ;
Soon swiftly dissolving, their crystals descend
   To deluge the earth with a glory of green.
But tread now with patience the pathway of duty,
   Nor darken all joys with a sorrow that's done ;
May each trembling tear on the eyelids of beauty
   Like bright April showers but herald the sun.
     Begone, dull repining, &c.

Sing, haste thee, lone sorrow, unfold thy dark wings,
   Like dreams of the past be thy fast fleeting form,

A love rudely blown in the first blast of spring,
  Will yield thee no sheltering arms from the storm.
Love, vast as the heavens, is round us and o'er us,
  Each floweret swings low 'neath its chalice of dew ;
Hark ! birds from the greenwood are singing in chorus,
  Be off with the dream-life, and on with the true.
    Begone, dull repining, &c.

# MAGGIE.

TAKE all the blue of Scottish bells
   Beside the streamlets pure,
The blue that in the heaven dwells,
That tints the waves or paints the shells,
   And Maggie's eyes are bluer.

Shake all the snow-down from the thorn,
   And Maggie's brow is whiter;
The reddest buds in summer born,
The rowan ripening with the corn—
   Her lips and cheeks are brighter.

Take all the sweets of summer bowers,
   That bend and blush to meet her,
Bejewelled with the sparkling showers,
The luscious fruit, the honied flowers,
   And Maggie's smile is sweeter.

Though time should take these charms away,
   And blasts of sorrow blight her,
Though snows of age upon her fall,
'Twill leave a heart that's worth them all—
   Far purer, sweeter, brighter.

# CHRISTMAS.

### SONG.

WINTER dons his dazzling crown,
  Icy diamonds quaintly glow,
Autumn's garb of russet brown
  Lies 'neath the pearly snow,
Scarlet-breasted robin sings
  Blithe upon the glistening spray,
Youth and age, sire and sage,
  Meet to hail the merry day.

  Sundered hands unite
    Round the Yule-log bright ;
  Banish care and sadness
    From our thoughts to-night ;
  Let the good old song
    Wake the echoes still ;
  Peace to all on land and foam,
    Hearty right " good-will."

Song and jest and music gay,
  Golden hours their wings unfold ;
Jetty locks will turn to grey,
  But love will ne'er grow old ;

Strife is vanquished, malice dies,
  Sweetly all the minstrels play ;
Lead the march 'neath the arch
  Twined with holly green and bay.

  Sundered hands, &c.


Earth, put on thy bridal robe ;
  Calm night, wear thy jewelled tire ;
Round the cycle of the globe
  Love flies on wings of fire.
" Christ our King was born to-day,"
  Loudly the anthem swells !
" Joy to earth !" " Peace and mirth,"
  Ring the merry Christmas bells.


  Sundered hands unite
    Round the Yule-log bright,
  Banish care and sadness
    From our thoughts to-night ;
  Let the good old song
    Wake the echoes still—
  " Peace to British hearts and homes,
    Hearty right good-will."

## WINTER, WILL YE NO GAE WA'?

Winter, will ye no gae wa'?
  Taigle here nae langer wi' us ;
Flowers are glintin' through the snaw—
  A'e bit glisk o' simmer gie us.
Tulips warslin' through the green,
  Crocus buds—ye've nearly drooned them—
Shake their heads and steek their een,
  Draw their gowden tippets roond them.

    Winter's stormy blast is blawin',
    Thrifty farmers maun be sawin' ;
    Folk are weary, ane an' a'—
    Winter, will ye no gae wa'?

Lassies, ye had little thocht
  Lippenin' to his yowrie glimmer ;
A' yer lichtsome braws are bocht,
  Lawn an' lace an' flowers o' simmer.
Noo wi' fickle shine an' shower,
  A' his days are spent in teasin' ;
Lauchin' at the drookit flowers,
  Lingel't locks an' feathers freezin'.

    Winter's stormy blast, &c.

Tricklin' teardrops fa' like rain,
   Bonnie bairns their mithers plaguin',
Press their heids against the pane,
   Wae an' weary for yer wa'gaen.
Eerie glints the amber licht,
   Hail is dirlin', rain clouds shoorin' ;
Spring's young birds hae a' taen fricht
   Wi' yer rattlin' an' yer roarin'.

Winter's stormy blast, &c.

## "A VANISHED HAND."

Come, list to me, the old man said,
  In accents soft and low,
For visions of the days long fled
  Dance in the fire's bright glow ;
A hand that tunes the harp of gold
Has touched me, as in days of old—
    An angel's hand.

And still, when silent hours oppress,
  I feel its pressure " there !"
Upon my brow, with fond caress,
  And nestling 'mongst my hair ;
And on the restless wing of love
It flutters round me like a dove—
    That gentle hand.

Oh ! what an influence, what a power
  On life's wild battlefield ;
How oft unseen in evil hour
  'Twas stretched to help and shield.
But when by wealth and honour blest
The world grew empty, for I missed
    That little hand.

From dreams, alas ! we wake to weep ;
" Sad heart, be strong, be still,"
For soon with joy my soul will leap
To feel its pulses thrill.
What bliss again to hold so much—
" All Heaven" descending, when I touch
That vanished hand.

## THE IMAGE MOURNS.

WHEN Bacchus toomèd his whisky stills,
And stoups ran owre in reamin' rills,
And hearts forgot life's cares and ills,
  Wi' rapture throbbin';
O' a' the airts the wind can blaw,
The siller melted like the snaw,
And men were brithers ane an' a',
  And "prood o' Robin."


Weel busk't wi' wreaths in George's Square,
Abune the street lamps' amber glare,
He scanned the crood wi' wistfu' air,
  Oor Poet Plooman.
And 'neath the bay-leaved glistenin' croon,
His sun-bronzed lofty broos cam' doun,
And settled in a sullen froon
  Maist thrawn and human.


At length richt howe the image spak' :—
I little ettled to be back,
Forjeskit, drookit, weird, and black
  As ony moudie;
But little dreamed I, when on earth—
Bad luck attend sic graceless mirth !—
Ye'd make the day o' Rabbie's birth
  A drucken rowdie.

"I've gaen a gate I dearly rued,"
That peck o' maut that Willie brewed
Aye devastates the land I lo'ed
   Baith late and early.
"Puir man, he mak's himsel' to mourn,"
I ken that brawly, tae my scorn,
For noo the fruits o' barleycorn
   I'm reapin' sairly.

But callous cuifs I aye disdain,
Wha sit owre Burns makin' maen,
And grind and grab illgotten gain,
   And rin to bank it;
I asked for bread, they gied me stanes,
I wroucht for't, for the wife and weans,
And noo there's naething left but banes,
   And Guid be thankit.

Wha dodge and deal in quirks o' law,
Tae ding the weakest to the wa',
And tramp puir brithers, when they fa',
   Are nocht to Rabbie;
I carena though 'twere Prince or laird,
Wha kept a puir dumb beast ill-fared,
And you, puir chiel', the tramway guard,
   Ill peyed and shabby.

But think na I've nocht guid to reap;
My gratitude is pure and deep
When mithers sing their bairns to sleep,
   Sweet Afton chantin';

Or lassies lilt fu' sweet and true
Some rhyme wreath dreepin' wi' the dew,
I listen, and my heart is fu'—
    There's naething wantin';

Or by some blink in ingle neuk
Some ploughman brither reads my book ;
Or Scottish shepherd, wi' his crook
    Among the cattle,
Rests in the shade owre Burns to pore,
Sees truths he never saw before
To help him in the rush and roar
    Of life's stern battle :

'Tis then my raptured spirit knows
The bliss of Heaven's grand repose ;
For Scotia's weel my heart o'erflows
    Wi' love untellin'.
Change, waefu' change ! when snaw-wreaths drift,
Nae pitying angel in the lift
But kens the eerie " Twenty-fifth "
    By oath and yellin'.

Noo, dinna tak' my words amiss,
The wey to honour Burns is this :
His birthday haud, to help and bless,
    Ye'll a' enjoy it.
Set richt some puir misguided chiel',
For duddie·bairns and mithers feel
In heart and pocket, and 'twill heal
    Your stricken poet.

# CHRISTIAN WARFARE.

LET Christians fail not in the fight,
   Nor think the battle long ;
For if 'tis hard to do the right,
   'Tis harder to do wrong.
Then forward, let the truth be known—
The friend of Jesus is his own.

How great his loss, in age or youth,
   What language can express,
Who for vain pleasure barters truth,
   Or counts it valueless.
How small his profit for the whole—
To gain the world, and lose his soul !

What though by direful ills assailed
   We press to gain the prize ;
Though oft our victories are veiled
   From erring human eyes ?
For us the Lord was once oppressed—
The proud man's scorn, the scoffer's jest.

Oh ! then, be brave in holy strife,
   In Christ we cannot fall ;
Withhold not talents, gold, or life,
   For He is worth them all.
Yea, worthy, worthy is the Lord ;
His service is a rich reward.

## THE LOST COIN.

My flitting fancy oft supplies
That picture drawn 'neath Eastern skies,
  Wherein our Lord portrays
A lesson simple, yet so grand—
A woman searching, broom in hand,
  With wistful, eager gaze.

Hark in what plaintive tones she speaks,
With troubled brow and flushing cheeks!
  Again she seeks the spot,
And bends her candle to the floor,
To search where she has searched before,
  And grieves to find it not.

The household cares, her daily pride,
Now for a space are set aside,
  When, lo! with glad surprise
She spies the coin; her task is crowned,
She calls her friends and neighbours round:
  " Rejoice with me," she cries.

Thus man is lost in paths unknown,
And thus the Saviour seeks His own;
  And when the lost is found,
Though dust its real worth conceals,
What words can paint how rich He feels
  When golden harps resound.

Oh, wretched man ! how sin impairs
The glorious image that he bears—
   He faints beneath his load.
But never with His own to part,
The Saviour clasps him to His heart—
   The image of our God.

The Priest and Levite passing by,
His joy behold with wondering eye ;
   But He who sorrowed most,
Through loss derives His richest gain,
Who rent the Temple veil in twain,
   To find what He had lost.

Put on thy festal robes, O earth,
With heaven unite your songs of mirth,
   Responsive to His call ;
When He who bore the Cross alone,
From desert wilds brings back His own,
   His joy He gives to all.

## THE TEMPLE OF THE HEART.

O LORD, we own Thy right divine !
The temple of the heart is Thine.
In holy wrath each image spurn,
The money-changers overturn.
In deep dismay Thy Spirit grieves
To see Thy house a den of thieves.

O sacred temple of the heart,
Which man has made a common mart,
Where heavenly gifts are bought and sold,
Where wranglers barter truth for gold,
Be hushed ! the Lord demands His own ;
He bought with blood each precious stone.

Majestic in His grief He stands,
This Temple was not made with hands ;
But rais'd by power divine and grace
To be His own abiding-place :
Meet home for happy angel guest,
By heavenly calms and glories blest.

They gathered round when Jesus shed
His tender tears for Lazarus dead,
And heard that bitter wail when set
The golden sun o'er Olivet ;
But who within Thy blest abode
Shall brook Thy wrath, O Lamb of God ?

Go cast abroad the Gospel seed,
And let the Word be preached indeed ;
Let Jesus' tears in pity flow,
Through human eyes for human woe,
Till all the powers of sin are dumb,
And Christ's eternal kingdom come.

# ARISE! FAINT HEART.

WHY sigh with vain regrets and idle tears,
  O'er sins we own forgotten and forgiven ?
Arise ! faint' heart, dispel thy gloomy fears,
  And take with joy the grandest gift of heaven.

Why longer gaze along the bygone track
  O'er hours misspent to murmur and complain ?
Will bitter sighs ere waft one moment back,
  Or blinding tears blot out one guilty stain ?

Say ! who shall charge, since God hath justified,
  Thy ransomed spirit with one sinful blot ?
And who shall take, since Jesus Christ hath died,
  Thy liberty by such a Saviour bought ?

Oh ! would we sigh, be this the vain regret ;
  Were all these tears for others' sorrows shed,
Like pale sweet pearls 'mid burning rubies set,
  They'd shine in fadeless glory on thy head.

Arise ! faint heart, God's promises are sure ;
  Still onward press, though enemies may frown ;
Like soldier good, with hardihood endure—
  The world thy cross—till heaven thy labour crown.

G

# SHALL I FORGET?

When loss is crowned by heavenly gain,
  Life's sun in cloudless glory set,
The blight of care, the toil, the pain—
  Shall I who lived forget?

Shall I, who faltered in the strife,
  Its terrors by experience proved,
Gaze o'er the battlefield of life,
  And think of it unmoved?

Shall I, who know the gain of loss,
  With battle past and arms laid down,
Forth from the shadow of the cross
  Not point them to the crown?

Shall I, betimes in wanderings lone,
  Hear mingled voices from the shore;
And shall the songs they sing be known
  To thrill me nevermore?

My heaven! thy highest bliss is crowned
  When sundered hands and hearts are met;
The love that life nor death has drowned—
  Shall I who loved forget?

Where dearest, tenderest memories throng,
　One cup of water cool and clear,
Ten thousand deeds forgotten long
　By earth are cherished here,

Where He who lived and died to win
　From death and shame our highest bliss,
Flings o'er the awful gulf of sin
　A deep forgetfulness.

# THE MEEK. '

PSALM xxii. 26.)

WITH honours crown the meek,
 Ye shining minstrel bands,
Ye spirits bright, who day and night
 Obey your Lord's commands.
From pain and conflict safe,
 Refined through flood and flame,
Earth passed them by, while the heavens high
 Were ringing with their fame.

One pitying Eye looked down
 When sorrows fell with years,
And ills increased till the heart had ceased
 To find relief in tears.
Alone, yet not alone,
 When mighty deeds were done ;
The Lord was near when never a cheer
 Proclaimed the battle won.

Ye heroes earth hath crowned—
 Ye foremost in the fray,
Who scorn to yield in battle-field,
 And cannot brook delay :
Say, could you stand and wait,
 Brave, silent, like the meek ?
Or bear the blow from friend or foe,
 And turn the other cheek ?

Oh, satisfaction pure !
   Oh, service most sublime !
Wide as the sea, their influence free
   Breaks o'er the sands of time ;
Long ere the last be first,
   Or tears of sorrow dried,
Heaven rings with mirth, for the lowly of earth
   Are deeply satisfied.

# KING JESUS CAME.

He came not with a proud array
Of glittering hosts and courtiers gay,
None thronged Him round with courtly bow,
No diadem adorned His brow,
No heralds trumpeted His fame, ˙
When meek and lowly Jesus came.

And yet, where'er His footsteps pressed,
He gave the faint and weary rest ;
He came for others' woes to weep,
To bid the dead awake from sleep.
To heal the sick, and blind, and lame,
The loving, lowly Jesus came.

And those who knew Him best could tell
He loved the little children well,
And gently stroked each baby head ;
" Forbid them not to come," He said,
For such must learn to lisp His name—
For such the loving Jesus came.

And yet He wandered sad and lone,
Although the world was all His own,
And went at midnight hour to pray
In lonely, dark Gethsemane ;
For those who oft deny His name
The loving, lowly Jesus came.

And oh, how patiently was borne
The world's cruel, bitter scorn,
And never in His glorious eyes
Would vengeful looks of passion rise ;
To feel our grief and bear our shame
The loving, lowly Jesus came.

And love was all His life below,
And in His death of dreadful woe
He cast on all around, above,
A look of everlasting love :
That love might be His name and fame
The loving, lowly Jesus came.

## "O YE OF LITTLE FAITH."

W<small>HY</small> should the Christian's star of faith
  Be dimmed by dark despair ?
Behold ! a cloud of witnesses
  Have filled the earth and air.

Brave hearts, who fought through shot and shell,
  Their glorious battles won,
Now strike their glittering harps to tell
  Great things our God hath done.

" Our God is ever strong to save,
  Our God is ever nigh ;
He clove the Red Sea's crested wave
  With pathway broad and dry,

" By which, with faltering steps we crossed,
  Reviewing from the shore
Where Pharaoh and his warlike host
  Had sunk to rise no more.

" When hungered sore, the manna sweet
  Fell from the midnight sky ;
The Jordan fled before our feet,
  When rolling broad and high.

" When thirst had parched our pilgrim band,
   His mercy, ever sure,
Procured, 'mid desert's burning sand,
   Cool streams of water pure.

" We saw His mighty arm dispel
   The fierce, avenging foe ;
And heard the thundering crash when fell
   The walls of Jericho."

Why longer tremble, " little faith,"
   Before life's troubled sea ?
The path where Israel's millions passed
   Is broad enough for thee.

Shall waves of doubt no more be crossed,
   From rocks the rivers run ?
Shall He whose arm upheld a host
   Fail now to shelter one ?

Hold fast each promise ; thou shalt see
   God more than all fulfils,
Nor think one billow of the sea
   Can whelm when Jesus stills.

## "THY WILL BE DONE."

LORD of all life, the strength and stay,
Star of our night, Sun of our day,
O guide Thy children when they say
    " Thy will be done."

Should wakeful conscience bid me pine
O'er trifled hours that once were mine,
It was my will, O Lord ! not Thine—
    My will was done.

Should vanity my thoughts engross,
Till want abounds with pain and loss,
Then help me, Lord, to bear my cross—
    My will was done.

Should sin and selfishness impair
A face and form that once were fair,
Then never let me breathe this prayer—
    " Thy will be done."

Should whispering envy work me woe,
And vengeful malice lay me low,
Then never by Thy hand, I know,
    Was evil done.

## "THY WILL BE DONE."

O Love ! so long misunderstood,
So blurred by man and misconstrued,
What comes from Thee alone is good—
  Thy will be done.

Still o'er Thy suffering children bend,
The Brother-Man, the sinner's Friend,
Till earth's with angel voices blend—
  " Thy will be done."

# THE ANGEL'S MISSION.

METHINKS, when on the rushing wind
    The angels stoop to help and cheer,
Some seraph marvelleth to find
    So much of heaven here ;

So many precious gems that throw
    Their lustre through the mist and mire,
And make this vale of tears to glow
    With beams of mystic fire.

The wealth of worlds above is here :
    True heroes, martyrs, kings uncrowned,
Whose voices charm their listening ear
    With sweet familiar sound.

E'en here, 'mid anguish, strife, and scorn,
    The dawn of peace its lustre flings ;
And heavy cares are lightly borne
    On love's celestial wings.

E'en here, in change, and death, and time,
    In fading form and fleeting breath,
Live faith and hope, and truth sublime,
    And love that conquers death.

They come ! in snowy, shining throngs,
    With blissful tidings long withstood ;
While man is looking for his wrongs,
    The angels find the good.

## DEDICATED TO PRINCIPAL MORISON.

FIRM on the Rock of Truth, behold !
    The Union lighthouse star
Flash out in gleaming shafts of gold
    To light the mariner,
When tempest-tossed, and almost lost,
    Amid the wintry blast ;
Right o'er the reef of Unbelief,
    Its warning beams are cast.

Around it angry seas have dashed
    Their billows, breaking white ;
The winds have wailed, the lightnings flashed
    In lurid lines of light ;
This silent form, 'mid calm and storm,
    Bright glimmers from afar—
And God be praised, glad eyes are raised
    To bless our Union star.

Heaven guard him now in life's decline,
    Who sought in early youth
To shed the light of love divine,
    By building on the Truth.
His soul is blessed when through the mist
    The ship, once near aground,
Is spreading sail to greet the gale,
    And speeding homeward-bound.

Shine forth, revolving hallowed ray,
  To all thy light is free,
Refulgent as the king of day,
  Unfettered as the sea.
Oh, shield the brave by land and wave,
  For many, near and far,
Are hastening home across the foam,
  By the light of the Union star.

# I WANT TO LIVE ALWAY.

I WANT to live alway :
  Oh ! hasten the day
Death's languishing phantom
  Shall vanish away.
The sweet, holy pleasures
  Of days that are o'er,
Have filled me with longing
  To taste them once more.

I want to live alway,
  And triumph o'er wrong ;
Though sinful and tempted,
  In Christ I am strong :
A glorious future
  My pilgrimage cheers,
Though dimly distinguished
  Through weakness and tears.

I want to live alway,
  And Hope beats so high ;
Though sorrows beset me
  I long not to die ;
By Christ reinstated,
  With Heaven my dower,
I ne'er was created
  To fade like a flower.

But why call it living ?—
    If God were unknown,
'Twere death to encounter
    Life's warfare alone.
If deep in my spirit
    His image I bear,
Wherever I wander
    My Heaven is there.

I want to live alway,
    For all that is dear—
For love everlasting
    And friendship sincere ;
For all I have learned
    In this schoolroom below
For all that I'm learning
    And longing to know.

# THE HIDING PLACE.

Where, oh, where shall I hide ?
  The Lord is seeking me ;
I long to fly from His searching eye,
  But whither shall I flee ?
I fled to the Tower of Pride,
  Made fast its bolts and bars ;
But it fell at last in a wintry blast,
  And I stood 'neath the gleaming stars.

I built a castle high,
  Without the corner-stone,
By day and night I toiled away
  To make it all my own ;
But soon the lightning flashed,
  I heard the thunders roar :
Ah ! works are vain, 'twas rent in twain,
  And the Lord was at the door.

I hid in a wood of Doubt,
  A maze of tears and sighs,
But round about the flowers peeped out,
  And God was in their eyes ;
He breathed through all the trees,
  His whisperings thrilled the air ;
I fled in haste to a desert waste,
  But found Him everywhere.

II

Oh ! earth, thou hast no place
   To hide—by wave or sod ;
No, never a rest for souls distressed
   Who seek to hide from God ;
But Goodness followed hard,
   And Mercy found my track,
And foot to foot in hot pursuit
   They ran, and brought me back

To love, and peace, and life,
   My sinful fear confessed,
All swathed about from care and doubt,
   To the Heart that loved me best ;
Where, o'er the blight of sin,
   His righteous robe He flings,
And from the storm I'm safe and warm
   'Neath the shelter of His wings.

## "GO! WORK TO-DAY."

I SHALL say, " His way is best,"
When unerring records show it,
And the ends of earth shall know it ;
When the heavens sing and shout it,
None will question, none will doubt it :
O'er the pathway backward gazing,
   Rapt and praising,
I will sing with throbbing breast,
  " Jesus' way is best."

I shall say " His way is best,"
I who loved my own, and doubted,
When the righteous cause seemed routed ;
Yea, when no one bids me show it,
Weeps, and longs, and thirsts to know it ;
When the poor no more are pleading,
   Rich unheeding—
Truth shall ring from east to west,
  " Jesus' way is best."

I shall sing, " His way is best,"
With a heart no longer aching,
When the long-lost chord is waking,
Where no gloomy haunted place is,
No chill graves, and no chill face is,
When the vanished hand is thrilling,
   Strong yet stilling ;
But no gems will crown my brow
  If I'm silent now.

## HE THINKETH OF ME.

To-night, when dear children are saying their prayers,
    All over God's Kingdom below,
My voice in thanksgiving shall mingle with theirs,
    For Jesus would miss me, I know.
Though none here may gaze on His beautiful face,
    Like the children who climbed to His knee,
I'll lay me to rest with the thought I love best—
    That Jesus is thinking of me.

His thoughts I can trace, here in woodland and dell,
    In earth, and in ocean, and sky,
When fragrance is borne from the sweet snowy thorn
    That nods 'mong the green branches high.
Lo ! the stars He upholds in night's dusky folds,
    In number how many they be !
Yet, wonderful thought, I'm never forgot,
    He careth and thinketh of me.

Then not for the honours that conquerors win,
    Nor crowns of the ransomed above,
Nor for terror, that " Death is the wages of sin,"
    I'll praise Him and serve Him for love.
For I could not be happy if Jesus were sad ;
    From sin and temptation I'll flee,
Lest a shadow should rise in the glorious eyes
    Of our Lord as He thinketh of me.

## "FATHER, TAKE MY HAND."

WEARY wandering to and fro,
I without Thee cannot go
Through this changing path below—
    Father, take my hand.

All untrod my journey lies ;
Clouds at morning oft arise ;
Thou art loving, strong, and wise—
    Father, take my hand.

Here are flowers in bright array,
Rippling streams, and sunshine gay ;
I may loiter by the way—
    Father, take my hand.

When I leave the verdant glade
For the forest's gloomy shade,
When the flowers of hope all fade—
    Father, take my hand.

Shield me, hold me, clasp me tight,
In the day as in the night ;
Round my weakness cast Thy might—
    Father, take my hand.

Let me not, by sin beguiled,
Leave Thee on the mountains wild ;
Monsters may devour thy child—
                    Father, take my hand

When my feet no longer roam,
And the light across the foam
Streameth from my long-loved home—
                    Father, take my hand.

## "IT IS I."

In every path of life
  I have a Guide and Friend;
In every scene of strife
  My Saviour will defend.
Oh ! Lord, when Thou art near me,
  All danger I'll defy,
As long as I can hear Thee
  Say gently, " It is I."

How sweet to walk with Thee !
  Thy wondrous love how dear !
Though on the raging sea,
  I cannot, will not fear.
O'er billows wildly rolling,
  And tempests rising high,
I'll hear Thy voice consoling,
  " Be not afraid, 'tis I."

When joy with gilded wing
  Sheds light and love around,
When gay and beauteous Spring
  With verdure decks the ground ;
In murmurs of the river,
  In trees that wave and sigh,
I hear the gracious Giver
  Say softly, " It is I."

## THE SHEPHERD CAME.

As fading light proclaimed departing day,
   And night in starry state her mantle spread,
The Shepherd came and took a lamb away
   That oft within the pastures I had led.
No eye beheld Him come or disappear,
But well I know the Shepherd hath been here.

Yet, was it strange ?   I never saw His face,
   Or marked His form across the mountain drear,
Thro' death's dense mist no footprints can I trace,
   But well I know the Shepherd hath been here.
Through dark alarms and Jordan's ceaseless roar,
Safe in His arms the little one He bore.

The Shepherd came, 'twas but His own He sought,
   Which long since He had found when far astray ;
That priceless one His precious blood had bought,
   The gift He gave, He came to take away.
Oh, scattered flock, dispel your woe and fear,
Rejoice ; for lo ! the Shepherd hath been here.

The Shepherd came to heal, and bless, and save,
   And soon again on one of us may call ;
Say not, they sleep within the silent grave,
   Or death enshrines them in his gloomy pall.
May faith reveal the heavenly pastures near,
And whisper that the Shepherd hath been here.

# THE MASTER SLEEPS.

How oft in fancy's realms I soar
  O'er winding river, mount, and sea,
And reach, as evening gilds the shore,
    Blue Galilee.

And in a little bark I sail,
  Tossed high upon the heaving tide,
And seek, while gathering mists prevail,
    The other side.

Now breaks upon my wondering gaze
  A hallowed light, divinely shed,
Where low the heavenly monarch lays
    His weary head.

He sorrows, suffers, toils no more ;
  Sweet voices thrill His raptured soul ;
He hears not ocean's angry roar—
    Roll ! billows, roll !

Sees He the land where angels sing,
  The home he left for such as I,
The blossoms of eternal spring—
    The glorious sky.

.        .        .        .

"How can the Master peaceful sleep?"
    The terror-stricken seamen cry;
O'er our frail bark the breakers leap—
    "Help, Lord! we die."

His voice hath stilled the stormy swell,
    And, gazing o'er the wild expanse,
The wrathful waters rushing fell
    Beneath His glance.

The crashing thunders ceased to roll,
    And peace pervades each glassy wave,
And peace hath filled each troubled soul—
    Peace Jesus gave.

Still o'er the world His pitying eye
    An everlasting vigil keeps,
And never, now, when storms are nigh,
    The Master sleeps.

# ONE IN CHRIST.

Each hour the restless ocean rolls
   Her incense to the sun ;
The interests of ten thousand souls
   Are centred deep in one.

The tender blades that heavenward shoot,
   The leaves that bloom and fall,
Draw life and nurture from the root,
   And one is more than all.

Thus nature's works are richly twined
   With lofty thoughts, which show
How sacred are the ties which bind
   The family below.

If haply here we grieve in part,
   And wound with careless tread,
The pain that rends the throbbing heart
   Is measured by the head.

Then swift we stay our reckless pace,
   And view with sad surprise
The grief upon the Saviour's face,
   The anguish in His eyes.

Oh ! solemn life to live, when all
 May reap what one has sown ;
We cannot rise, we cannot fall,
 Nor joy, nor grieve alone.

And life's sweet lyre is oft retuned,
 While trembling tear-drops start,
Since we who love Him daily wound
 That tender, broken heart.

# AT THE GRAVE.

I STOOD amid the valley of the shade,
In awful silence, trembling and alone,
Upon the threshold of the great unknown,
Where beauty's blossoms shrivel up and fade,
And thrones and sceptres in the dust are laid ;
Alone I stood, affrighted and dismayed.
Here reigned the King of Terror, and around
His ancient throne, in dire confusion, lay
The fragments of the nations passed away ;
In wreck and ruin, hastening to decay,
No relics, save the dust of such are found,
As earth had fêted, idolised, and crowned.
Here hushed the tread of nations as they passed,
The din and roar of battle, and the clank
Of arméd warrior rushing from the rank ;
Here Pharaoh's foaming chargers plunged and sank ;
Unuttered horror, cavern deep and vast,
Of dead who wait the resurrection blast.
Cold mother earth, the first grave and the last,
And lo ! a radiance o'er the gloom is shed,
One grave alone is empty, and a form
Looms from the dusk, like sunlight after storm
An angel's smile, as brilliant and as warm,
Where lowly once reclined the Saviour's head.
" Fear not ! whom seek ye at the grave ?" He said,
" Why longer seek the living 'mongst the dead ?"

His eyes flashed light, and in their living glow
I saw the skull of Death amid the dust :
A broken sword, a shield begrimed with rust,
Lay severed by the victor's final thrust,
When raged wild war, and fell the fiercest foe
That ever conqueror in death laid low,
His mailéd helmet shattered at a blow.
Now from the dust unfading blossoms spring, .
And boughs immortal twine their leaves o'erhead ;
Along the path I hear the living tread :
" My soul ! it was thy Saviour who was dead,
Awake ! awake ! ye choirs, let heaven ring,
Where, grave's, thy victory ? where, death, thy sting ?
Rabboni, Lord, my Conqueror ! my King !"

# THE BIBLE.

THIS little Book, this priceless, precious gift,
    All joys combining;
A bow of light, when clouds of sorrow drift—
    A silver lining.

From ages dark, by time's rude waves uptossed,
    A world's great history;
Reviewing, now my loftiest dreams are lost
    In love and mystery.

In love unfathomed as the deep untold,
    Unknown for ever;
Through which with joy eternal life we hold—
    And who shall sever?

For earthly pleasures, fleeting as its dreams,
    But make thee dearer;
And every threatening wave of trouble seems
    To bring thee nearer.

Here is a spotless robe of righteousness
    I ne'er could merit;
And cool and clear a crystal stream to cheer
    My thirsty spirit.

Here is a light 'mid darkest shades of doubt
   That knows no waning ;
Here is a heavenly peace within, without,
   Fierce war maintaining.

Here to each passer-by I oft may tell
   Some strange, sweet story ;
Though tossed about by sin and suffering fell,
   An heir of glory.

'Neath smiling skies and dazzling clouds uprolled
   In blue expansion,
Secure and fixed by title clear, I hold
   A heavenly mansion.

And, stranger still, ere sinks the golden sun
   O'er death's broad river,
A crown of fadeless honour may be won,
   Or lost for ever.

Eternal shelter, dark o'ershadowing rock,
   Grand and commanding—
Time's rolling seas and the elements' rude shock
   Shall leave thee standing.

# ZACCHEUS.

WHEN at eve the freshening breeze
 Swayed the branches bending o'er,
Jesus walking 'mongst the trees
 Passed beneath a sycamore.

Dreamful fancy oft supplies
 Light and language to the scene :
How Zaccheus' searching eyes
 Scanned Him through the leafy screen.

Heedless of the Levites' frown,
 Swift he stayed the human tide :
" Friend," said Jesus, " hasten down—
 At thy house I will abide !"

Downward from the verdant height,
 Flushed with mingled pride and shame,
Trembling with suppressed delight,
 Quickly to his Lord he came.

Thus they passed along the way,
 Many murmuring the while ;
Some with lofty looks and gay,
 One with sad and holy smile.

Silence filled the banquet hall,
  Hushed the song and mirthful jest ;
Wonder lit the eyes of all—
  Fixed upon their Royal Guest.

Shame the wayward bosom burns,
  New-born thoughts and hopes arise,
While each wandering glance returns
  To the heaven of His eyes.

Lord ! the half of all I hold,
  Since my house Thou hast not loathed,
I will freely give in gold
  That thy poor be fed and clothed.

Lord ! thy love-inspiring ray
  Deeper than Thy wrath shall burn ;
What I falsely took away
  That fourfold I will return.

And the Saviour bending o'er
  Saw afar the accomplished plan ;
Felt the sinner's guilt no more,
  When He clasped the brother man.

Love upholds His grand renown,
  Still His call is full and free ;
Friend Zaccheus, hasten down—
  Jesus would abide with thee.

# QUESTIONINGS.

Whom seekest thou, oh world?
Wild, tossing, heaving world,
Remorseless, cruel, cold, and bitter world ;
Rolling thy dark, deep waves,
All ridged with fleecy foam,
Beating in majesty.
Thy billows break, they break,
Rise wrathfully, and break
Against God's mighty bars.

God, give us God,
Echoes each sobbing wave,
Mutters the thunder deep,
Utters the mountain grand,
Thunders the avalanche,
Rustles the golden leaf,
Whispers the falling snow,
Murmurs the storm-tossed soul—
God, give us God.

Whom seekest thou, oh world?
Gay, laughing, merry world,
Green, waving, singing, loving, glowing world,
Wondrous, poetic world,
Fair art of God star-spangled, glittering world ;

Waving thy myrtle boughs,
Singing thy songs of joy,
Decking thy path with flowers,
Wearing thy crown of stars.


God, give us God,
Ripples each silver wave,
Murmurs the river deep,
Whispers each glossy leaf,
Quivers each blooming flower,
Trills from the soaring lark,
Trills through the mossy wood,
Echoes a child's sweet voice—
God, give us God.

## WATCH WITH ME.

In the morn, when life was glad,
  Earth looked fair as summer's smile ;
Saith the Saviour, I am sad,
  Watch with me a little while.

Clouds across the blue were cast,
  Shadows fell along the years ;
To Gethsemane we passed
  Through a maze of grief and tears.

Far from laughter, light, and mirth,
  Ceaseless night obscured the day,
Where the busy sounds of earth
  Seemed so strange and far away.

Lions met us in the way,
  Terrors vanquished by His grace ;
Fainting at His feet I lay
  In that dreary desert place.

Shrank my trembling heart within,
  When my heavy eyes "unsealed,"
Saw the penalty of sin
  In His agony revealed ;

Heard that awful, anguished cry,
    Ringing through the darkened years ;
When He sought from such as I
    Human love with human tears.

Take, oh earth, thy tawdry joys,
    I have glorious company ;
Take them, I have made my choice—
    Jesus through Gethsemane.

Here my chastened soul at length,
    Plunged within a depth of grace,
Weakness perfecting in strength,
    Saw my Saviour face to face.

Watch with Jesus, sad one, now,
    Here fulfil His blest commands ;
Wipe the death-dew from His·brow,
    Heal the nail prints in His hands.

See him plead, in weeping eyes,
    From the cities' alleys vile ;
Hear thy Saviour when He cries—
    Watch with Me a little while.

## ANGELS.

HANDS that tune the harp of gold,
　　Angel hands I used to clasp,
Touch me as in days of old,
　.　Let me feel your living grasp ;
We your songs of hope require
When you strike the golden lyre.

Eyes that view fair Eden's bloom,
　　Gentle eyes serene and mild,
Visit earth's low, darkened room,
　　Where the light has seldom smiled ;
Eyes that wept in days of yore,
Come and weep for love once more.

Voices lost to us so long,
　　Jasper walls no echoes wake,
Leave the choir of seraph song,
　　Through the stars your journey take ;
Angel voices singing glad ;
Can you sing, and earth so sad ?

Ears that hear the songs on high,
　　Ears that were so swift to hear ;
Hear ye not earth's woful cry ?
　　Are you far, or are you near ?
Oh ! the songs, the voices dumb,
Pattering feet that never come.

Hearts in yonder glorious sphere,
　　With the ransomed safe and blest ;
Countless souls are dying here,
　　Do you live in perfect rest ?
Heaven, with starry eyes aglow,
Speaks in thunder ! Never ! No !

# THRICE TRIED.

ALL night they toiled, and when the rising dawn
Shot rosy glimmers through the dusky sail,
And morning voices whispered in the gale,
The weary fishers knit their sun-bronzed brows,
As through the furrowed deep their vessel ploughs;
They 'mid the ceaseless rocking and the spray
All night had toiled, but naught at morn had they.

Lo ! one descries a form upon the shore,
And while he turns to gaze his spirit grieves ;
His bosom, like the troubled ocean, heaves ;
" Oh ! blue Tiberias, thou art ever lone,
And dark and dreary since our Lord has gone ;"
Hark ! 'tis a voice borne on the rising tide—
" Cast down your net upon the other side !"

With haste the nets are cast into the deep,
Though how, or why, they hardly understand :
But all bestirred themselves at the command ;
And never yet saw fisher such a take,
While fish like silver sleet the waters flake ;
A circling eddy round the frail bark laves,
From one, a swimmer strong amid the waves.

Low at the Saviour's feet enrapt he kneels,
And wakeful memory must needs recall
The solemn silence of the judgment hall,

And those sad, speaking eyes that pierced him through,
When loud and shrill the cock at morning crew ;
'Twas thou ! who left Him with the rabble horde,
And thou ! who thrice denied thy captive Lord.

Simon, thou son of Jonah ! lovest thou Me ?
Yea, Lord.   Then feed My lambs : I hear them bleat ;
And " Lovest thou Me ?" the Lord does twice repeat ;
And Peter casts his eyes across the deep,
While waves of strong emotion o'er him sweep,
Unheard the sea-mews' shriek, the breakers' hiss ;
Yea, Lord, Thou knowest all things,
And Thou knowest this.

# WHAT THEN?

My hopes are bright, the young man cried,
  The morn of life is fair,
Of all its varied joys untried
  I mean to have my share;
The page of life before me spread
  Is writ with golden pen;
Come hither! son, the old man said,
  And let me hear it, then?

In fortune's smile I mean to bask,
  And brilliant honours gain,
Perhaps 'tis rather much to ask,
  But there's something in a name.
A yacht, with snowy sails outspread,
  I hope to own; and when
You tire of that, the old man said,
  Pray! what, my son, what then?

I'll bid farewell to ocean's spray,
  And turn my thoughts to home,
Upon a gallant steed and gay
  O'er hill and dale I'll roam;

Or I may build a mansion high
 By some romantic glen ;
And gaily did the old man cry :
 A mansion high, what then ?

I'll woo and win the fairest maid,
 Some pretty village belle ;
And wandering 'neath the hawthorn shade,
 A tale of love I'll tell.
And then, of course, I mean to wed,
 As do the most of men,
And earnestly the old man said :
 You mean to wed, what then ?

I hope by then broad lands to own,
 And mingle with the great ;
My humble voice may yet be known
 In Council Halls of State.
Or as a judge, full wise, may I
 The ruthless rogues condemn ;
And softly did the old man sigh—
 And what wilt thou do then ?

I then must grow quite frail and old,
 With locks as white as snow ;
My step no longer firm and bold,
 Shall feeble grow and slow.
And then, you know, we all must die,
 It is the lot of men ;
And sadly did the old man sigh—
 And what wilt thou do then ?

He turned, and from the old man went,
　No answer could be given ;
To him a life of pleasure meant
　No treasure up in heaven.
But all day long, with aching thrill,
　That voice came back again,
And whispered in the midnight still—
　Ah ! what wilt thou do then ?

## ADVENT OF SUMMER.

Hark ! Heaven's loud acclamation, " It is done,'
   The woodlands flourish in their native green ;
A brighter glory glitters in the sun,
   And floods the mountains with a golden sheen.

I hear the brooklets laughing as they greet
   The tangled brushwood on their rocky way ;
I hear the lambkins from the meadow bleat ;
   The rivers make a murmuring melody.

Fresh on the boughs the hawthorn bud appears—
   Spring's bridal wreath amid her dark locks worn ;
The flowers that wept are smiling, and their tears
   Like dewdrops glistening 'neath the glance of morn.

From viewless vaults above the grassy mead
   The skylark's song the busy farmer hears ;
While chilling gusts disperse the copious seed,
   By faith he views the drooping golden ears.

Thy works all praise thee, Lord, by day and night,
   They utter forth Thy mercies, freely given ;
Pale Luna's rays which burn so mildly bright,
   And stars that tremble on the verge of heaven.

Awake ! awake ! let hearts and voices sing
   To Him who clothes the earth with verdure fair ;
Ten thousand hearts bound at thy voice, oh spring,
   Ten thousand songsters thrill the balmy air.

## THE WILL AND THE WAY.

Come hither, little Adelaide,
And tell me why that thoughtful shade
   Rests on your brow to-day ;
The smile that wreathed your lips has flown.
Teacher ! you say, 'tis hard to own
   The will and not the way.

A will so strong, yet never know
The luxury of soothing woe,
   When giving would be gain ;
To see life's ills, yet bear no part,
With nothing but a loving heart
   That only feels for pain !

Why ? nothing but a heart ! I cried,
'Tis more to God than gold thrice tried,
   The wealth of worlds above ;
He brought no more who came to give
Eternal life to all who live,
   And conquer all with love.

And then I told her how He came,
And dwelt on earth in woe and shame,
   To bear the ills we dread ;
Who, though the sparrow had her nest,
On earth or ocean found no rest,
   Nor where to lay His head :

And how it grieved His spirit pure
To see the sufferings of the poor,
  Oppressed by evil powers ;
What waves of sorrow o'er Him swept,
When for humanity He wept—
  And all His grief was ours.

Go forth, thy priceless gifts bestow,
Poor, making many rich below,
  Be thine that better part ;
Till Christ His life through thine diffuse,
And teach thee by His grace to use
  Love's diadem—a heart.

## SONG OF LIBERTY.

*(DEDICATED TO THE RIGHT HONOURABLE WILLIAM E. GLADSTONE.)*

Son of Britain, lion-hearted,
   Be the guardian of our laws,
Fearless as the brave departed,
   Suffering in a noble cause.
By the honours that have crowned you,
   By our dauntless heroes' graves,
Rise and right the wrongs around you—
   Armed resistless like the waves.

*Refrain*—No surrender ! no surrender !
        Still 'tis Freedom's battle-day ;
        Heaven defend you, victory send you,
        As you stand for Liberty !

Break the arrows of oppression,
   Laurels still with life are bought ;
What a measureless possession
   Is the liberty of thought !
Flashing far, by vale and mountain,
   Words of peerless wisdom go ;—
Bearing, from your heart's clear fountain,
   Healing tides for human woe.

*Refrain*—No surrender ! &c.

K

Here are tyrants, rise and chain them !
   Vice and want are rampant still,
Ills like fiery chargers, rein them—
   Bind them with an iron will.
Faith with angel hosts attending,
   Hope exultant lead the van ;
Fervent prayers to heaven ascending—
   Speed the hero and the man.

*Refrain*—No surrender ! &c.

## MYSTIC VOICES.

Blue eyes, dark and tender,
　Thou hast, little Jim ;
But their lustrous splendour
　Oft makes others dim.
Voices, sad and lonely,
　Whisper, when they shine,
White-robed angels only
　Have such eyes as thine.

Locks of auburn lustre
　Thou hast, little Jim :
O'er thy brow they cluster,
　'Neath thy sun-hat's brim.
Lips the rose outvieing,
　Smiles of witching grace,
Find us ofttimes sighing—
　" 'Tis an angel's face."

Linger with us, darling,
　In this world of woes ;
Earth hath need of angels,
　Heaven overflows :

But those voices, dearest,
　　Whisper soft and low,
That the songs thou hearest
　　Only angels know.

*Refrain*—Darling ! thou art dearer,
　　　　Fairer every day ;
　　And we clasp thee nearer
　　　　Lest thou flit away.

# LIFE FOR A LIFE.

TOLLING so slowly,
Chiming so lowly,
　Over the strife,
Over the judgment hall,
Over the church spire tall,
.Sadly the deep bells call—
　" Life for a life."

Chaplain attend him,
Warder befriend him,
　Down-stricken youth ;
Guilty ! we knew it !
Oh ! how could he do it ?
But sadly he'll rue it—
　" Tooth for a tooth."

Chatting at dinner
Over the sinner,
　Wretch ! let him die !
Few here will care for him,
Prison cold fare for him,
Put up a prayer for him—
　" Eye for an eye."

Oh ! the deep pain of it,
Bearing the strain of it,
   Bitter and wild ;
Pleads not a friend sincere,
Father or brother here,
Was he a mother's dear
   Innocent child ?

Oh ! the sad rueing,
Never undoing
   What has been done ;
Death's solemn sleep for him,
Others must reap for him,
Sorrow and weep for him
   Under the sun.

Pity him, Heaven !
All unforgiven,
   Bearing his load ;
All here is vanity,
Holy profanity,
Safe from humanity,
   Speed him to God.

Land of the beautiful,
Home of the dutiful,
   Hark ! o'er the strife,
Tolling so slowly,
Crushing so lowly
All that is holy—
   " Life for a life."

# LOST AND FOUND.

HE lost a smile of winning grace,
Which broke like sunshine o'er his face,
Sweet relic of a babe she nursed,
His gentle mother missed it first.

He lost a glance serene and bright,
Shot fearless from a depth of light ;
A carol, heard when evening fell,
His brother missed—he knew it well.

He lost a care for others' weal,
He ceased for others' woes to feel ;
And, losing heart and self-respect,
His time was lost, his talents wrecked.

. . . .

He found earth's promise false and vain,
Her smiles flit past, her tears remain ;
An evil round of bitter sweets
The crown of misery completes.

He found not 'mongst the giddy throng
One hand stretched forth to right the wrong ;
And retribution for the past
Wailed round his spirit like a blast.

E'en human love grew strange and pale,
Droop'd down and withered in the gale ;
Sin's dark abyss before him lay,
And terror taught him how to pray.

Pursued to Calvary's cross by fears,
His wounds too vile for human tears ;
The purest clasped him to His breast—
The Man of Sorrows gave him rest.

The saddest heart that wept below
Revived his joy and soothed his woe ;
By bleeding hands his wounds were bound,
Where sins are lost and souls are found.

# CALDER WOOD.

OH ! Calder Wood, I love thee !
　Thou art near in every dream,
Thy dark o'erarching branches,
　Thy rippling, gladsome stream ;
Like strains of far-off music
　I hear the voices still
Which made thy sombre depths resound
　And echo to the hill.

I hear a sweet song ringing,
　I see a happy smile,
A face of wondrous beauty
　I loved and lost awhile.
Bright eyes 'neath waving tresses,
　Where love and laughter shine ;
Blue as the heaven peeping down
　Through spreading beech and pine.

The shy wood violets quiver,
　The verdant brackens stir ;
The happy birds are singing
　From yonder stately fir.
And darker, swifter, deeper,
　I see the water glide ;
While little feet are gleaming white
　Beneath thy sparkling tide.

Alas ! 'tis but an echo
From joyous days long gone ;
No more those voices thrill thy bowers
With laughter or with song ;
But from thy purest flowers
A dewy wreath I'll twine
For one who left thy leafy shades
For grander bowers than thine.

# THE SAILOR'S FAREWELL.

I go, he said, o'er the sounding deep,
Where wild waves swell and tempests sweep,
And the maiden sighed, and turned to weep
　　By the rocky, shell-strewn shore.
As dew-drops clung to the salt sea flowers,
She clung to his arm in the parting hours,
　　And wept, for her heart was sore.

I go, he said, but this heart of mine
Like living ivy clings to thine,
The image of thy form divine
　　Upon my heart I'll bear;
The snow-wreath melts when the south wind blows,
And, dearest! when the buds unclose
　　The blossom thou shalt wear.

Farewell, my dear, my own sweetheart,
We can be true though far apart,
Whate'er betide, where'er thou art,
　　I'll ever think of thee;
The waves roll back to the sandy shore,
The spring returns when the frost is o'er,
　　And the tar comes back from sea,

# ANOTHER.

"I wont! I wont!" said Ella Brown;
  "You wont!" exclaimed her mother;
Then listen, dear, you wont be here,
  For I shall get another
Good Ella Brown, who will not frown,
  And tease her little brother;

A merry, gentle, little Miss,
  Who'll sit in Ella's chair,
As sweet and gay as a June day,
  With Ella's eyes and hair;
A laughing Miss, who'll get your kiss,
  And eat your supper there.

Your pretty dolly shall be hers,
  And hoop and ball and pever;
She'll help mamma, and never ba,
  And say "I wont!" to grieve her;
Your muff and furs shall all be hers,
  And your hat, your Sunday beaver;

And she shall do my will at once
  Without a fret or frown;
She'll learn to spell and write so well,
  And never be put down!
She'll come at once, and be no dunce,
  My little Ella Brown.

Your dear papa will pat her head,
  And I will comb her hair ;
She'll kneel, too, down in your night-gown
  With mild and reverent air,
And lay her head on Ella's bed
  When she has said her prayer.

" She wont ! mamma, I'm growing good,
  See now I will begin,
I'll learn to spell my lessons well,
  And then the prize I'll win ;
I'm growing good ! I wont be rude,
  Oh ! do not let her in !"

# DUTY.

Duty woke me from my dreaming,
  Bade me leave the path of pleasure,
When the sun of joy was beaming;
  And he gave me toil for leisure.
Come! he cried, no time for laughter—
Duty first, and pleasure after.

Hopefully I turned to follow,
  Pleasure waits for care and sorrow,
Hills arise beyond the hollow,
  Joys from tears their lustre borrow;
Come! he cried, no time for musing—
Duty first must be your choosing.

Duty, stern and righteous master,
  Now with conscious pride I own thee,
But thou hast a meaning vaster—
  I had fainted had I known thee
When you called me from my dreaming,
When the sun of joy was beaming.

O'er the path of duty bending
  Pleasure sought me, found me singing,
Prayers of gratitude ascending,
  Roses from the desert springing;
For I found a hidden treasure,
Duty done is lasting pleasure.

## CHILDHOOD'S WONDER.

How oft in childhood's happy days
  My wondering heart would cry—
What hid'st thou from my longing gaze,
  Oh ! summer evening sky ?
Like silver sea aflowing,
With golden waves aglowing,
  Tints roseate hue and sunny blue,
What keep'st thou me from knowing ?

What hid'st thou from my longing gaze,
  Oh ! darkling, frowning sky ?
With awe I see the lightning's blaze,
  So swift, so bright, so high,
White clouds by strong winds driven,
And rolling thunders riven ;
  What hand unseen hung this fair screen
Betwixt the earth and heaven ?

What hid'st thou from my longing gaze,
  Oh ! star-bejewelled sky ?
Eternal suns, whose glories blaze
  Too bright for mortal eye.
Bright gates that gleam and quiver,
Green fields by life's pure river ;
  Loved ones who sing before the King,
And live in joy for ever.

# DUPLICITY.

WHAT baleful art, with winning wiles
The unsuspecting oft beguiles ;
What strikes us in the heart, and smiles ?—
   Duplicity.

Spite, malice, envy, all agree
Before thy shrine to bend the knee,
Since all their evils meet in thee—
   Duplicity.

So sweet, so fair, we could not trace
Base falsehood on thy beaming face,
Else we had fled from thine embrace—
   Duplicity.

E'en Lucifer himself might blame
This rival who usurps his fame,
When Beauty's ruby lips proclaim—
   Duplicity.

Environed by thy subtle lure,
The poor seem rich, the rich seem poor,
Yet both agree they cant endure—
   Duplicity.

Here truth is sold at any cost,
And love affects to hate the most,
And cruel hate makes love her boast—
      Duplicity.

This treacherous one in candour dressed
When wounding says 'tis for the best ;
None could more fervently detest—
      Duplicity.

Though oft Religion's mask is worn,
The rose still hides the bristling thorn,
Hearts broken, reputations torn—
      Duplicity.

May heaven from all thy snares defend,
Till thy doomed spirit shall descend
To depths we cannot comprehend—
      Duplicity.

# WOMAN'S RIGHTS.

## A Dialogue.

FREDERICK,  
WILLIAM,    } MEMBERS OF A FIELD CLUB.  
RICHARD,  
FRANK,

MARIA, SISTER TO FREDERICK.

UNA, HER FRIEND.

*Scene*—STUDY.

*Enter* MARIA AND UNA.

*Maria.* This room is worthy of minute inspection,
Walk in ! walk in ! you'll find there's no
deception.

*Una.* Your brother's study ! these shells are beautiful,
and what a marvellous collection.

*Maria.* Our Fred and other members of the Club
Are now at large in search of worm and grub,
Great beetles, spiders, caterpillars, clegs,
Snails, hornets, butterflies, fish, birds, and eggs.

*Una.* I think we'd better go now, Maria, dear,
I hope he doesn't keep the beetles here ;
But see ! what curious stones !

*Maria.* These all come handy as he toils along:
A piece of coal, flint, lime, stone, iron, and
glass—
The meanest weed that grows he wouldn't pass.

*Una.* Hark! who comes?

*Maria.* My brother and his chums;
Quick! Una, we will hide.

*Exit* MARIA AND UNA.

*Enter* FRED, WILL, DICK, AND FRANK.

*Fred.* What news?

*Will.* Our worthy Secretary's looking glum.

*Frank.* They've sent their compliments, and cannot
come.

*Dick.* The ladies!
That ends our pic-nic!
For well the ladies know that if they cannot
come, we cannot go.

*Frank.* I think, to say the least, 'tis most unkind;
To thwart our pleasure they have all combined.

*Fred.*　Have ye not marked of late some signs of
　　　　　revelry at Brenton Hall,
　　　　Which gathers all the maidens round, our sex
　　　　　excluding ?
　　　　Some mischief broods, I doubt not, 'mongst the
　　　　　fair,
　　　　Which bodes no good to those who are not
　　　　　there.

*Will.*　I bet 'tis woman's rights.

*Dick.*　Which is another name for woman's spites.

*Fred.*　Our Maria's in the plot, and, for a wonder,
　　　　Goes to the Hall through pouring rain and
　　　　　thunder.

*Dick.*　What sport to hear this dark conspiracy !

*Frank.*　This brave deed can be done :
　　　　There's Sarah Jane, my cousin Una's maid,
　　　　She'll find for us some sweet secluded shade,
　　　　Where we will hear, and view, and masquerade.

　　　　　　*Exit* FRED AND FRIENDS.

　　　　　　*Enter* MARIA AND UNA.

*Maria.*　Ha ! my brave soldiers, is your scheming done ?
　　　　Our simple part has never yet begun.

*Una.*  Alas! for deeds of love by worldlings viewed,
Our Dorcas work is sadly misconstrued.

*Maria.*  Yet, what say you, if every girl unites
To give our guests a raid on woman's rights?
Devote the night to lecturing—in brief—
And hold them captive in this vain belief.

*Una.*  Their own nets take them for a living prey;
What happy fortune led us here to-day?

*Maria.*  Come! heads together, 'tis a glorious plan;
Suppose we head our subject, What is Man?

# PART II.

*Scene—*BRENTON HALL.

DORCAS CLASS.

*Enter* MARIA AND UNA.

*Maria.*  Sweet sisters, how I hail the social hour
Wherein we seek to raise our fallen power,
And pour on tyranny our discontent;
I will not idly prate, like vaunting man,
That I was pressed and cajoled to the chair,
But truly let me own how proud I am
To occupy this place;
And, as the wingèd moments haste away,
I will be brief, concise, and to the point;

Nor copy man—uncourteous, selfish, vain—
Who, all forgetful of a brother's right, raves on
    unceasing.
Be brave ! my sisters, forward to the fray,
For man has robbed us of our lawful right,
Because his jealous mind has felt our sway.
In Literature, in Music, and in Art,
In all things noble save his strength,
Which owned is but a sorry boast ;
For as a stream with devious, noisy splash
Beguiles the passing traveller by its din,
To think some foaming torrent hasted forth
Impetuous to the sea :
Thus, boasting his superior strength, man shows
    his weakness ;
All mighty powers are silent.
Lo ! the stars, the golden glowing sun,
The pensive moon, how silently they shine ;
And woman, fully conscious of her sway,
Silently pursues the tenor of her way.
Permit me now to call Miss Una Vann
To introduce the question—
" What is Man ?"

*Una.*    The Psalmist was a man of wisdom great,
And keen poetic insight.
'Twas he who called this question to the light,
And, 'neath the mystic glory of the night,
In deep humility exclaimed—
" Lord ! What is Man ?"

First seen, the lordly creature is but small,
Yet does his coming cause more grateful joy
    than our poor selves ;
Unwelcome waifs we come to cot and hall.
Thus first he comes, content a time to nestle,
His life depending on the weaker vessel.
Next seen, he is avowed a household pest, and
    nurtured from his infancy to think himself
    superior to our trodden selves.
He comes ! deep discord brooding on his brow—
Brawls with the maid, or bids his sister haste,
Kicks the good dog, and pulls the kitten's tail,
Ignores his gentle mother's weak protest,
Who stands as though afraid to rest her limbs
In his most august presence.
Oh ! sisters, 'tis a sight most pitiful,
In this our civilised and lovely land—
A grief so common that no pity wakes the dead
    heart of the world.

*Maria.*    Most ably has our sister, dear Miss Vann,
Discussed this weighty question—
" What is Man ?"
His origin more clearly do we see,
Which dim foreshadows what he yet may be.
With pleasure now upon Miss Wood I call :
Convener of the work at Brenton Hall.

*Miss Wood.*    The monster, as portrayed in early stage,
Gives promise of his traits in riper age ;

Behold ! the maniac Prig, with learnèd airs ;
The bold young man who struts, and winks,
    and stares ;
The crusty Bachelor, with manners rude ;
The drawling Fop, the Dandy, and the Dude ;
In various forms and colours he appears
For football, cricket, yachts, and volunteers.
Beware ! ye maidens—trustful, innocent, and
    unsuspecting—
Thieves are they, for they steal most ruthlessly
The tint of soft carnation from the cheek,
The light of laughter breaking from the eye ;
And, when our hearts are stolen,
How they flit from drooping flower to flower,
Or, like an Indian chieftain from the war,
Whose boast is of the many scalps that hang
Around his horrid girdle,
The modern lover wears his hearts instead,
And vaunts the number.

*Maria.*　Miss Wood's dramatic power could scarce be
    beat,
Her speech is quite an intellectual treat ;
When each and all their hearty thanks accord,
I'll call upon our sister, Anna Ward.

*Miss Ward.*　Now view a wooer fond, who scarce can see
His sweetheart's hand encumbered with a straw,
But swift relieves with many compliments ;
And, should a stone or stile-impede her way,

Behold ! how gallantly he carries her,
How gently sets her down.
Witness the same in hapless wedlock bound,
When years but few have touched her thought-
　ful brow
With silver streaks, which gleam like snow in
　summer ;
Like ivy clinging round a blighted tree
Her fretful babes around her garments hang,
The infant which upon her breast reclines
Moans piteously ;
Yon lordly savage, basking in the sun,
With daily press extended in his palms,
Chides at their din, and hastens forth at eve
　for unmolested quiet ;
No grey hairs streak his glossy, raven pate,
Nor shabby garment decks his portly form,
Nor lines of care deface his beaming brow,
Nor trace of shame for wreckage of a life
He swore to love and cherish.
Alas ! how soon the flame to ashes turns—
A woman's heart when won how small the
　boon !
What find we cheaper in our native isle
Than woman's faithful heart ?
Home fiends and outdoor seraphs are they all,
But we will plot their doom at Brenton Hall.

*Maria.*　To solve the question—
　　　What is Man ?—in brief,

A cruel-hearted coward and a thief ;
Miss Anna Ward his shallow heart has spanned,
And touched her subject with a master hand ;
That woman is his mate, and something more,
Will be maintained by sister Jeanie Orr.

*Miss Orr.*  Oh ! had I language that I might portray fair
   woman's influence breaking from the
   homes,
Where, crowned by heaven, and dowered by
   right of love, she reigns :
Herself a queen, in heart and mind,
By Nature more exquisitely designed,
More heavenly in her grace.
Who strikes the first impression of great
   thoughts,
Which wing their way like arrows o'er the
   earth ?
Who crowns the poet with his laurel wreath,
And tunes his harp to mighty melodies
And deep, soul-searching sounds ?
First here to bid us welcome to the world,
And sing our infant lullaby,
To clasp the cherub's hands in evening prayer,
And kiss the wound that smarts ;
To scatter light abroad, yet, like the sun,
Retain her peerless lustre.
First here to hasten forth in peril's hour,
And yield her life up for the child she loves,
And last to soothe the wreck of blighted hopes ;

When threatening waves leap high and terrors
    rage,
Last, and alone, she stands ;
Last at the sufferer's side,
With cool, pale hand upon the aching brow.
Oh ! peerless woman, beautiful and brave,
Last at the Cross and foremost at the grave ;
I marvel not that woman's soft, pale hand
Should move the central forces of the world ;
But this hath caused me wonderment,
That she, exposed to ills and cruel wrongs,
Should have no voice by voting here wherewith
    her wrongs to right.
Shame ! on man's laws, which bear no trace of
    woman's power most elevating ;
Shame ! let the voice of conscience echo shame !
Forward ! brave sisters, let our power be known,
Be woman's right the right to hold her own.

*Enter* FREDERICK, WILLIAM, RICHARD, AND FRANK.

*Maria.*  What means this bold intrusion ?

*Will.*  Our injured reputation we would save,
    And answer to your charges, which are grave.

*Una.*  They come here to sustain their dying cause ;
    To hear them, sisters, is to break our laws.

*Fred.*   A cause that dares not scrutiny is weak.

*Una.*   But here we suffer not a man to speak.

*Fred.*   Your vain discourse discreetly held from view
          The man who mated with the bawling shrew,
          The henpecked wretch beneath a tyrant's rod,
          Who looks for rest and quiet 'neath the sod ;
          The gossip, who the rabble crew regales
          With idle tattle, while her infant's wails
          Greet the sad father as he homeward hies,
          His bosom rending with its helpless cries.

*Frank.*   Then there's the gadabout, who, in her way,
           Neglects the poor man's home, and spends his
                pay,
           His children tattered, shivering from the cold—
           Poor, weak, neglected lambs, without a fold ;
           His home the relic bare of better days—
           No goodwife's smile, no ingle's cheery blaze.

*Will.*   The heartless beauty, with her witching wiles,
          The (dangerous flirt, with dimples, smirks, and
                smiles,
          The husband-hunter (always in the van),
          Who modesty resigns to play the man,
          The sweet-voiced nightingales who ply their
                arts
          To prey on rending sighs and broken hearts,
          The vain coquettes, the scheming painted hags,

Who net us with their chaff and money bags ;
When on the downward track I do deplore
That woman is his mate, and something more.

*Maria.* Be woman's word the last, our lawful right,
If deep her fall, 'tis from a loftier height.

*Dick.* Ungrateful fair, how can you thus forget
You owe to dear papa a filial debt,
Who always pays for every fond caress
With jewels, laces, parasols, and dress ;
Who shields the lovely girls with all his heart,
And, when he knows they're wrong, can take
their part?

*Maria.* Your reckless words from truth and reason stray,
Bold sirs, begone ! there's danger in delay.

*Will.* Oh ! banish not for ever from your sight
A miserable moth who loves the light.

*Fred.* Retreat, ye wingless Angels, to your bower,
And henceforth know your weakness is your
power ;
Why tread in hostile legions, rank and file,
Who vanquish men and heroes with a smile?
For truly do we find, when summing all,
That faults are found on each side of the wall ;
While pleasures bring their complement of care,
I recommend that each from strife forbear.

*Maria.*   Agreed ! We all adhere, on one condition—
        That you befriend the fund of this our Mission.

  *Fred.*   Aid Woman's Rights—an imposition !

*Maria.*   Nay, brother, aid a humble Dorcas Mission,
        Since you have all declared that woman's rights
        Is just another name for woman's spites.
        Come, shield your fellow-creatures from the
            cold ;
        What here you give returns a thousandfold.

*Frank.*   Capricious woman, fashioned to deceive,
        True daughter of your prying mother, Eve !

*Maria.*   That adjective your case exactly fits.
        Eavesdroppers call us, and I hold we're quits.
        Behold ! a man who freely will admit
        That he was vanquished by a woman's wit.

  *Una.*   Hand round the money box !
        In mercy's cause your gracious ears incline—
        To err is human, to forgive divine.

  *Fred.*   Hold ! not a dime, unless you promise here
        To grace the pic-nic with your light and cheer.

*Maria.*   To this we all consent,
        Since you have frugal minds, on pleasure bent.

*Una.*   Oh, thanks, a thousand thanks !

*Maria.*   Let each and all their hearty thanks accord !
      And quickly to a ploughshare beat the sword.

*Una.*   And now let social pleasure be our guest,
      And music charm and soothe each ruffled breast.

*Dick.*   And let us have a waltz, wer't but to show
      We bear no malice to the witching foe ;
      Now hand-in-hand a gay triumphal arch,
      See Will and Marianna lead the march.

*Una*   I'm sure with all their nonsense and their noise
*to Maria*   What were the world without them ?
*(aside.)*   " Bless the boys !"

## MITHER SCOTLAND FLYTES.

AULD mither Scotland, sichin' sair,
   Ae day began to flyte and grummel ;
If I've been prood, quoth she, I'm sure
   Oor pride aye gangs afore a tummel ;
   I've got enough to keep me hummel
     And laigh this day.

Oh ! my puir bairns, ye're sair misleard
   To brag sae muckle o' yer glory ;
Take tent nae, for I'll no be sweart
   To clip the wings of Whig and Tory,
   And tell the world anither story
     Ere fa's this day.

Thae trashy foreign sangs ye're skirlin',
   Whene'er ye meet wi' ane anither,
Hae set my very teeth a-dirlin' ;
   And losh ! the wey ye ca' me mither
   It fair upsets me a'thegither
     To hear't this day.

Ye independent ! truth to tell,
   In bonnie Scotland's far-famed nation
There's hardly ane wha kens himsel'
   In manners, dress, or conversation,
   But on the reefs o' imitation
     Is lost this day.

Some e'en their liberty wad tine,
    Puir slaves, tae fashion, gowd, and drinkin';
And gin they get some dorbie's mind,
    Wha's words hae weight wi' siller clinkin',
    'Twill save them e'en the fash o' thinkin',
      Themsel's, this day.


What's common-sense, noo, wantin' siller,
    What bonnie face or gowden tresses?
When ills o' every shape and colour,
    Sair wrangs, dire hardships, and distresses,
    Are winket at through gowden glesses
      By Scots this day.


Tho' much o' Burns's muse ye brag,
    The carl wi' drouthie cronies spreein'
Could brawly off ye tak' his wag,
    And ca' yer haivers nocht but lecin';
    A toomstane jist the maist ye're giein'
      For worth this day.


Ye sing a " Man's a man for a',"
    The countryside and neighbours deevin',
And think he's no a man ava;
    Nae mair yer silly sel's deceivin',
    Jist sing he's better dead than leevin',
      If puir this day.

M

And while there's Scotchmen douce and leal,
 And housewives eydent, tosh, and handy,
There's mony a feckless ne'er-dae-weel,
 And weel I wat there's mony a randy,
 And mony a thowless, glaiket dandy,
  . Ca'd Scotch this day.

And lassies that wi' sic forgether,
 The path o' honest duty shirkin',
Gaun gamphin', busk't wi' flower and feather,
 At dancin' sprees till midnight lurkin';
 They leave their dowie mithers workin',
  Puir slaves this day.

Oh ! were ye a' as guid as brave !
 Whaur muckle's gien I muckle ettle,
And no because ye're like the lave,
 But made o' very different metal;
 Oh ! wad ye tak' a thocht and settle,
  Be wise this day.

Then stop thae bagpipes, blawin' snell,
 Auld Scotland's heroes need nae wheezin';
Dae something worthy o' yersel',
 And tent ye, tak' a word in season,
 And gin ye think yersel' worth pleasin',
  Be Scotch this day.

## THERE'S WEALTH IN THE OLD
## WORLD YET.

I HEARD a voice with hollow sound
  Exclaim, The world is done;
There's nothing good can ere be found
  Beneath the glowing sun.
Come friend, I cried, your search renew,
  'Tis hardly time to flit;
Your search renew, you'll find 'tis true,
  There's wealth in the old world yet.

I heard a voice in dire despair
  Proclaim, all love for good
Has left the world without a prayer,
  To die in solitude.
I asked a mother, Is it true?
  She said No! not a whit;
She clasped her child, and singing smiled,
  There's love in the old world yet.

I heard a sigh which plainly said
  Bright honour now is gone,
And every spark of truth has fled,
  Dire falsehood reigns alone.
A maiden cried, 'Tis quite untrue,
  Such thoughts I can't permit;
My lover's true, your search renew—
  There's truth in the old world yet.

I heard a whining voice exclaim,
  No joy in all the earth ;
And happiness is but a name,
  A myth, a dream is mirth.
I asked a schoolboy, and he laughed,
  And cried, with merry wit,
You're all at sea, just look at me,
  There's joy in the old world yet.

I heard a low, despairing wail,
  " Like withered leaves we fall !"
Here all you try is sure to fail,
  The grave will end it all.
But Bethel's star amid the gloom
  By God's own hand is lit ;
Go, strive and wait, 'tis never late—
  There's hope in the old world yet.

# THE ANVIL'S DEFENCE.

[Uproar in a Church Concert owing to the appearance of an anvil at anvil chorus.]

OH ! merciless doom to chaos and gloom,
   From the sanctuary swift to be hurled ;
An anvil whose power but one fleeting hour
   Astonished the musical world.

From life's turmoil and rush to the deep solemn hush
   Of your sanctum you secretly brought me ;
While mystery sealed what the future revealed,
   And bitter experience taught me.

So gaily I sang to the hammer's loud clang,
   The sharpest of critics confessed it ;
My musical ears were deafened with cheers,
   But blowing one's horn I detest it.

The church looked askance,
I read in her glance
   An enmity cruel and bitter ;
My voice while I sang with irony rang,
   Mine eye had a cold, steely glitter.

Then her voice, stern and cold,
Through the edifice rolled,
   What meaneth this vile innovation ?
What led you to bring this unholy thing,
   Polluting our fair habitation ?

Avaunt, then ! quoth I, 'twere vain to reply,
  Such mean accusations don't harm me ;
For any one knows I'm ready for blows,
  And savage assaults don't alarm me.

But let me remark, if you had a spark
  Of gratitude left to rely on ;
You'd certainly be indebted to me
  For the beauty and strength of your Zion.

For who would repair your edifice fair
  If anvils were spiteful, like mortals ?
Each rivet and bolt would rise in revolt
  And topple your pillars and portals.

One lesson at best let my presence suggest,
  Ere swiftly to chaos I'm hurled ;
Let earth with her cares bring here for repairs
  The ruin and wreck of the world.

# REVIEWS REVIEWED.

*Linnet.* THIS book is full of fossil chimes,
Old motto songs behind the times.

*Swallow.* To common minds a mystic maze,
But born to shine in distant days.

*Owl.* The book is tedious, dull, and slow,
Poetic merit very low.

*Blackbird.* When reading, how the minutes fly,
Poetic merit very high.

*Rook.* This work is full of errors grave,
The author either fool or knave.

*Lark.* Here truth and poesy have met,
The work's a gem, divinely set.

*Robin.* Within are gems which shall endure,
But the get-up is very poor.

*Goldfinch.* A whited sepulchre without,
Within confusion, lies, and doubt.

*Eagle.* 'Tis void of wisdom, wit, and mirth,
And should be banished from the hearth.

*Parrot.*   'Tis void of wisdom, wit, and mirth,
            And should be banished from the hearth.

*Jackdaw.*  'Tis void of wisdom, wit, and mirth,
            And should be banished from the hearth.

*Crow.*     'Tis void of wisdom, wit, and mirth,
            And should be banished from the earth.

*Sparrow.*  The fool has neither wit nor fun,
            And should not live beneath the sun.

*Barn Fowl.* 'Tis full of wisdom, wit, and fun,
            And should not live beneath the sun.

*Albatross.* Each page the dazzled reader turns
            Reveals a Wordsworth or a Burns.

*Magpie.*   Each page the dazzled reader turns
            Reveals the shade of Robbie Burns.

*Cuckoo.*   Each page the dazzled reader spurns,
            He sees the shade of Robbie Burns.

*Goose.*    With rage the dazzled reader turns
            To see the shade of Robbie Burns.

            Let all who sail these treacherous seas
            Have ballast to outlive the breeze,
            Now basking in the blaze of day,

Now heart-chilled by the drenching spray ;
And happy, though he stand alone,
Who holds opinions of his own,
In whom no angry passions rise
When glaring misprints greet his eyes ;
Who knows amid the whirling maze
Coarse flattery from truthful praise ;
Who seeks for truth, though truth be stern,
And is not overwise to learn,
While chiming fools that cross his path
Invoke his pity, not his wrath ;
For everywhere the author finds
That many men have many minds,
And many minds beneath the sun
Save time and thought reflecting one ;
And critics, like the vulgar throng,
Are sometimes right, and sometimes wrong.

# HER SMILE.

HER eyes, I cannot tell their hue,
I know not whether grey or blue ;
Her features, were they Grecian pure ?
Well ! they were beautiful, I'm sure ;
Upon her head some silver streaks
Gleamed 'mid the dusky pile ;
I know not why I loved her so,
But this remains, I surely know,
She had a heavenly smile.

It flashed along the lines of care,
And caught reflections everywhere ;
Like search-light gleaming through the night,
The secret heart-wound brought to light.
It thawed the frost of Pride ;
And thoughts in love's perennial sun
Came out and blossomed, one by one,
Like flowers opening wide.

And ever since I hold it truth,
That never from the eyes of youth
Flashed love on lightning glance so kind—
Babe innocence was left behind ;
Blue eyes and tresses bright,
Young beauty from the field retires ;
For oh ! 'twas formed 'mid burning fires,
That diamond blaze of light.

And languid eyes from life's despair
Found hope and solace shining there,
And turned from midnight watchings lone
To heaven, the source from whence it shone;
For after bitter showers
Such smiles are broken lights of love—
God's sunbeams scattered from above,
To light this world of ours.

# THE LITTLE ARM CHAIR.

THESE twenty long years in silence I've stood,
If my voice reach your ears, pray ! don't think me rude ;
I once was quite new, though now old, worn, and bare ;
What I'm telling is true, said the little arm chair.

I was bought when the flowers were budding to bloom,
And placed in a neuk of a bright little room ;
When a rosy queen came, who was wond'rously fair ;
Two years she did reign in the little arm chair.

And then when the tall trees were withered and thin,
And the late harvest sheaves were all gathered in,
And the flowers of spring had been long since dead,
A sunny-haired queen came to reign in her stead.

As long as I live I ever shall mind
How the first little queen was so loving and kind ;
She stepped from the throne with a dignified air,
That Sissie might reign in her little arm chair.

And the second queen reigned for many a day,
Yet no scars I sustained 'neath her peaceful sway ;
She was nursed in these arms with the tenderest care,
And she constantly loved me—her little arm chair.

But one bright, happy day, when June birds were singing,
And the sun o'er the earth all its glory was flinging,
A fairy queen came, with tresses of brown,
And beauty and grace was this maiden's crown.


I shall never forget her, nor the desperate feuds
When Sunny hair met her in menacing moods ;
In one dreadful affray I was all scratched bare—
There are marks to this day, sighed the little arm chair.


'Tis with love I remember one calm Sabbath morn,
That a fragile and tender young monarch was born ;
Yet he reigned quite supreme, and none ever would dare
To offend this young king of the little arm chair.


How oft to my visage a smile he would force,
When he made me his carriage, or called me his horse ;
And sometimes I hardly thought it was fair
To call me a donkey—his little arm chair.


Then I hailed with the flowers in the blythe month of May
Another young monarch, so handsome and gay ;
'Twas in vain I bemoaned, scarce his weight could I bear,
I creaked and I groaned, said the little arm chair.


And oft in convulsions my whole frame would reel
When he climbed on my back (as if I could not feel) ;
When questioned how came he so high perched up there,
He always did blame me—his little arm chair.

The next king that reigned was of strange dreamful mood,
But I oft thought his dreams never did me much good ;
For in solving some mystery by wonderful art,
Hè drove a strong nail straight into my heart.

He tied all the stools to my legs in a row ;
He made me a shop, and he made me a show ;
These wonders invented my health would impair—
He ne'er seemed contented to call me a chair.

How glad then to hold a queen in my arms,
With tresses of gold—quite a bundle of charms ;
Her reign was of pleasure, and never of care,
But another queen came to the little arm chair.

On this strange stage of life I had acted my part
As a pony, a carriage, a donkey, a cart ;
But soon 'twas a cradle, a dollhouse, a stair,
And when she was weary—a little arm chair.

Yet at this queen's caprice I never could frown,
Her eyes were so blue, and her hair was so brown ;
But my little love's reign was as transient as air,
For another king came to the little arm chair.

He plastered my arms with candy all o'er,
He made me a barrow to wheel on the floor ;
He sold me at last for a jargonelle pear,
And another king reigned in the little arm chair.

I hailed him with pleasure, my last little king,
For he was the fairest that ever was seen ;
The deeds of these monarchs go read and compare,
As recorded by me, said the little arm chair.

These ten kings and queens in succession all reigned,
Yet through all the turmoil I never complained ;
My motto was always with patience to bear,
Although I am only a little arm chair.

And now I am resting in peace from the strife,
I have set them all out for the battle of life ;
May their hearts be as pure and untainted by care
As they were when they reigned in the little arm chair.

## THE LADDIE I LO'E.

How can a Scotch lassie unblushingly tell
A secret she's keepit sae lang tae hersel' ?
Her love micht be great, and the lad micht be braw,
But whaur is the lass that wad own it ava?

> *Refrain*—'Twad waste ony laddie,
>          Ay, maist ony laddie,
>          Tae ca' him the flower o' them a'.

If my laddie were here I'd pawkily say :
" Wha thocht muckle o' him had little adae ;"
Though, quately, I ken he's kind-hearted and true—
But dinna lat on that I said it to you.

> *Refrain*—A wice-lookin' laddie,
>          A nice-lookin' laddie,
>          Aye leal is the laddie I lo'e.

Yet sometimes I wunner the laddie can stand
A lass wha's aye gien' him the back o' her han' :
" Come, lassie, and gree wi' a chap," quoth the chiel' :
" A kiss I maun hae, or ye'll learn me to steal."

> *Refrain*—" Sic claverin', laddie,
>          Yer haverin', laddie ;"
>          Quo' I, " Man, yer head's in a creel."

Yestreen by the burn I was sairly to blame,
He said he wad leave me, an' never come hame ;
I said that I wunnert he never had gane,
His bidin' or gaun were concerns o' his ain.

  *Refrain*—What says he, the laddie,
    O wae's me, the laddie,
    To think he wad leave me my lane.

" I'm leavin' ye, lassie," the bonnie birds sang ;
" I'm gaun," quo' the burn, as it rippled alang ;
I grat, for my love fairly conquered my pride ;
I leant on his shouther my blushes to hide.

  *Refrain*—" My haun' to ye, laddie,
    I'm gaun wi' ye, laddie,"
    An' soon he will mak' me his bride.

## SCOTIA, MOUNTAINLAND.

Scotia, mountainland, rugged and bold and free,
　　Peerless in beauty, unrivalled in charms ;
Artists have painted thee, poets have sung of thee,
　　Ocean hath circled thee round with her arms.
Flowers have been wreathed for thee, broadswords un-
　　sheathed for thee,
　　Deuse as thy forests, they flashed in the sun ;
Nations have fled from thee, heroes have bled for thee,
　　Fields have been red when thy battles were won.

　　　Dear to the wanderer's eyes, Scotia, thy hills arise,
　　　　Braving the tempest, and breaking the wave ;
　　　Wealth cannot buy for thee sons who can die for thee,
　　　　Scotia, mountainland, home of the brave !

Scotia, long were thy castles and palace-halls
　　Battered, through ages of peril and fear ;
Lowly the ivy leaves cling round their ruined walls,
　　Honour their ruins, in dust they are dear—
Kings have ascended them, heroes defended them,
　　Stormed from each fortress with valour sublime ;
Bravely they fought for us, dearly they bought for us
　　Laurels that bloom in the wreckage of time.

　　　Dear to the wanderer's eyes, Scotia, thy hills arise,
　　　　Braving the tempest, and breaking the wave ;
　　　Wealth cannot buy for thee sons who can die for thee,
　　　　Scotia, mountainland, home of the brave !

Heather-crowned mountain home, Heaven anointed thee,
  Sages predicted thy glory afar ;
First in the battlefield God hath appointed thee—
  Truth is thy buckler, and Freedom thy star.
Brave hearts unite for thee, daring the right for thee ;
  Wrong still is rampant, and Truth is obscure ;
Let us endure for thee, till we procure for thee
  Peace that is holy, and homes that are pure.

  Dear to the wanderer's eyes, Scotia, thy hills arise,
    Braving the tempest, and breaking the wave ;
  Wealth cannot buy for thee sons who can die for thee,
    Scotia, mountainland, home of the brave !

# RETURNED.

AND so thou hast returned to me,
Who sent thee from thine own roof-tree ;
And watched thee hence with secret joy,
E'en as a mother speeds her boy.

Pale, wan, and crushed, and travel-stained,
Disowned, defeated, and disdained ;
Thou'rt mine, though all the world should spurn,
Hail ! wandering dove, return ! return !

One heart will bear the final test,
Since thou on earth has found no rest ;
A martyr's halo gilds thy brow—
I never loved thee more than now.

The die is cast, the pang is o'er,
I never dreamed to see thee more ;
Still, worthless creatures bask in fame,
And merit bears the blight of shame.

Life's way is wildering and complex,
But love can cover all defects ;
No eye but mine can ever see
The glory thou wer't meant to be.

The spring returns when storms are o'er,
The wave returneth to the shore ;
These editors are cruel men—
My sweet spring poem back again !

# ROBIN'S KIRK.

*DEDICATED TO THE LATE ROBERT THOM, GOSPEL TEMPERANCE ADVOCATE.)*

DEAD ! man, Tam, I'm wae to hear it,
    Though I'm neither kith nor kin ;
For his mate for heart and speerit
    Robin hasna left ahin'.

Few among the great folk kent him,
    He had neither gowd nor lan' ;
But there's mony will lament him—
    Man he was an awfu' han'.

A' his life was spent for ithers,
    A' oor troubles were his ain ;
Treated a' the warld like brithers—
    Aye, man, Tam, and Robin's gaen.

Whaur he cam' by a' his knowledge
    Was a wonner far and near ;
'Twasna gotten in the college,
    Sae he said when folk wad speer.

Often hae I stood to hear him
    In the green at e'enin' mirk ;
Wee things croodin' to be near him ;
    This, said Robin, is my kirk.

Come o' every creed and section,
    Come, and bring yer sins and cares ;
Nane here waitin' for collection—
    This kirk never needs repairs.


'Twasna made by man's construction,
    It can stan' baith tear and wear ;
Heard ye nocht o' my induction ?
    Heaven ordained and sent me here.


Come awa', there's nae back-speerin',
    Sins I havena ance tae name ;
Faither sent me, and my errand
    Is to find and bring you hame.


Haud na up yer hands fornent Him,
    Beggin' aye for what ye hae ;
Losh ! it's plain ye havena kent Him,
    Or ye wadna treat Him sae.


Dinna mak' the saints think shame noo,
    For the poorest o' ye a',
Gin yer ne'er-dae-weel cam' hame noo
    Wadna send the lad awa'.


Naething ! naething ! stan's atween ye,
    Will ye bear this truth in mind ?
What ye're seekin' for was gi'en ye
    Eighteen hunner years sin' syne.

Tam, man, hoo the crood wad gether,
    Harkenin', round aboot they'd press ;
Cam' to hear o' Robin's Faither—
    Liket Robin's gospel best.


Ae nicht, when the crowd had gethered,
    Cam' an ill-faurt, drucken chiel',
Crying, Robin should be tethered :
    " Lads ! come on, we'll stane him weel."


Robin's look gaed through and through, man,
    Saw the carl on mischief bent ;
Guidsake ! quoth he, is that you, man,
    Sic a cheenge I never kent.


Aye ! and ye are Allan Wood, man,
    Bide, I'll keep ye weel in sicht ;
It's an ill wind blaws nae guid, man,
    Hech ! I hae a text the nicht.


Man, I kent ye when a callan',
    And yer dacent granny Reid
Wadna ken her braw wee Allan,
    Though she rose up frae the dead :


Wadna ken that voice sae husky,
    Frae the lips she used to kiss ;
Kent ye ever oucht like whisky
    To produce a wreck like this ?

Tent ye, Allan, bide a wee, man,
  Ye've a friend wha, I micht tell,
Thinks as meikle shame o' me, man,
  As yer thinkin' o' yersel'.

It's oor Faither takes yer part noo,
  Drives my logic to the wa';
Says, wha sees me micht take heart noo,
  Robin's in—there's room for a'.

Some folk here wha's aye done weel, man,
  Failin's dinna understand;
I can tell just hoo ye feel, man;
  Come in ower and gie's yer hand.

Hear the Word, and dinna doot it,
  Bring yer sin, and come awa';
God will think nae mair aboot it—
  Losh! He's no like us ava'.

# A CHILD'S FIRST LOSS.

*Child.*  MY grandpapa has left his staff down here,
How will he walk without it, mother, dear?

*Mother.*  He needs it not where weakness is unknown,
'Mid palaces of gold and jasper stone;
With joy he saw the Saviour drawing near,
Whose rod and staff did comfort him from fear;
Now safely passed from earth to heaven above,
He needs it not, my love.

*Child.*  Mother! he left his glasses in this case,
Without them once he could not see my face.

*Mother.*  But dimly through a glass he saw us here,
Now "face to face all mysteries appear,"
Undimmed by care, unsullied by a tear;
Of death his mental vision bears no trace,
His keen eye travels swift through time and space;
Grief fades in joy and sufferings all forgot,
Sweet child, he needs them not.

*Child.*  Mother! he left this book.  Yes, child, I know,
His bible was his guiding star below,
Of all things treasured here the dearest, best,
Which hath to man the Saviour's mind expressed.
"Come unto me ye weary, come and rest."

He heard, and conquering death, his mortal foe,
Swift hastened to the heart that loved him so ;
Yet, child, with this he never more can part,
'Tis graven on his heart.

*Child.*   And does he need no more his little Jim ?

*Mother.*   Yes, child, he needs us, we will go to him ;
Heaven's sweet, new joys efface not from his mind
The pressure of those arms that round him twined,
One tender look of love, one action kind,
Till love, the light of Paradise, grows dim,
No cherub chants like thee his evening hymn ;
If 'neath the skies my darling be forgot,
'Twill be when love is not.

# FAILED.

He passed our earthly way—a noble form along the busy
  street,
With gentle, toil-worn hands and weary feet,
  And locks grown early grey;
A princely heart from servile worldlings veiled—
Men knew him as a man whose life had failed.

Success before him fled, as rainbow fair at morn foretells
  the storm,
It reared o'er dire defeat its phantom form,
  While ruin round him spread ;
And friends, like moths that bask in fortune's light,
Led to the fray, and failed him in the fight.

This silently he bore, well knowing that for such is yet
  reserved
Deep censure from the Master whom he served,
  Nor scorned, but pitied more ;
Poor hearts on whom the curse of heaven falls :
" Woe ! woe ! ye graves unseen, ye whited walls."

Yet some true friends believed, bereft of social standing,
  gold, and friend,
That right e'en here would conquer in the end,
  And fortune be retrieved ;
This once he thought, but now full well he knew
Such doctrine in its essence is untrue.

The wealth of worlds above were wanderers ever, lone,
    downtrodden, spurned ;
They wept o'er wrong, their hearts within them burned
  A living fire of love ;
Poor, friendless, scorned, sore burdened, and oppressed,
The worldling's fool, the merrymaker's jest.

The cup was not removed, he drank it to the bitter dregs
    alone,
Loss, death, like billows over him have gone,
  And then, by sufferings proved,
Some loyal hearts who knew and loved him best,
Weeping, have laid him to his lowly rest.

Failed ! how the vaulted heaven rang out derisive, merry
    peals o'erhead,
When for the conqueror the feast was spread ;
  And life's grand crown was given
By One who fainted 'neath a heavier cross,
And bought our life with death—our gain with loss.

# SONG OF HOPE.

Look heavenward ! for behold ! the clouds have lifted !
  Presaging light at hand ;
So long upon the billows' crests we've drifted,
  We must be nearing land.
Truth comes through mist and doubt, though long belated,
  With faith more deep and strong ;
Hope hears the voice of joy that love awaited
  And lost so long ! so long !

So long Tradition's night and baleful error
  Have held despotic sway ;
The world is breaking from the reign of terror,
  The night must herald day.
The dew of tears upon our hearts is lying,
  And sighs have hushed the song ;
Behold ! the avenger comes ! who heard us crying—
  Oh ! Lord, how long ! how long !

Oh ! list, the long lost chord above is ringing,
  Where strifes and discords cease ;
The long lost hope across the deep is winging
  With olive branch of peace.
And hearts like flowers that droopt in winter's blighting
  Grow tranquil, brave, and strong,
To feel the cruel wrongs of earth are righting,
  Where love has lived so long.

# L E N A.

VIOLET eyes have lost their light,
Rosy lips are marble white;
Angels whispering in the night—
  Where has Lena gone?

Snowy hands we loved to press,
Eager hands stretched forth to bless,
Listless lie and motionless;
  Where has Lena gone?

Languishing her flowerets die,
'Neath the shadow of her eye,
Speechless hear our anguished cry—
  Where has Lena gone?

Hand in hand to school or play,
Was it only yesterday;
Have I loitered by the way?
  Where has Lena gone?

Side by side at evening hours,
Laden from the woodland bowers,
I have watered all my flowers;
  Where has Lena gone?

## LENA.

Fresh in youth and snowy fair,
Silken brown her flowing hair,
See her smile still lingers there ;
   Where has Lena gone ?

Still that angel face appears,
Calm and pure before our tears,
Smiling through the gloom of years,
   Where has Lena gone ?

Where the choral anthems ring,
Through the bowers of deathless spring,
Birdie, thou hast taken wing ;
   Lena there has gone.

# TWO WORLDS.

THE world, methinks, we live in two,
One old, the other always new,
One dreamland, and the other true ;
The one a world of sense and sound,
By touch and sight and feeling bound ;
The other high, serene, and chaste,
Where sound were but an idle waste.
Through realms of viewless thought we stray,
A thousand years are but a day ;
Truth, order, love, and joy are here,
And all that makes the old world dear ;
'Tis here, in letters clear and bold,
We read the history of the old,
The secrets of the earth disclose,
Where thought first breathed in swaddling clothes.
Yet, strange, the new world was the first,
The temporal at its breast was nursed,
Draws all its beauty, light, and force
From this unseen eternal source :
Each blade of grass, each drop of dew
Found shape and being in the new ;
But faithless creatures 'neath the sun

Affirm that there is only one.
Touch twig and flower and leaves that fall,
And sigh and murmur, this is all.
Oh ! could we use the temporal one
Like Jacob's ladder 'gainst the sun—
A lofty means to higher end ;
Go ! mount it, step by step ascend,
Till truth unveils the mystic scene,
And nought is common nor unclean.
Behold ! a child, while others play,
Who never saw the light of day,
To whom the flower, the field, the brook
Have ever been a sealèd book :
Yet in the sun his soul expands,
He stretches forth his little hands,
Plucks the fresh bud, inhales the breeze,
Feels all he loves, yet never sees.
'Tis thus the mortal blossom springs,
O'ershadowed by eternal things ;
For God we plead, for knowledge sigh,
But wings must grow ere we can fly.
Strange faces at the window peep,
Sweet voices call us in our sleep,
Though spoken low in undertones ;
We beat our hands against the stones ;
We call for lights, but God is wise,
And veils them from our infant eyes.
Those sounds, though vague and indistinct,
Have taught the untutored mind to think ;
But ever to the seeking soul

o

A goal that's won is not the goal ;
But soon the new world looms in sight,
As morn in waves of living light
Breaks glorious on the sands of stars ;
Our only glimpse is 'twixt the bars
Until we find the golden key,
Cast off our shackles, and are free.

# PROVIDENCE.

Ay, Jamie, lad, yer grannie's bairn the day,
I'm thinkin' but ye've had yer fill o' play ;
See ! there's a hassock for yer wee sair fit,
I needna tell ye no to leave the bit,
Gaun glaikin' barefoot aye by hill or howe ;
Ye're dune wi' schoolin' for a while, I trow—
Braw weel I ken ye're no that muckle carin',
Hech ! it's an ill wind blaws nae guid, my bairn.
When ye're an aulder lad ye'll hae mair sense,
Sic ongaun's nocht but temptin' Providence ;
When I was sic anither as yersel'
I hadna muckle playin', "mind I tell !"
My faither failed, and I was sent to wark,
Sair trailed till nicht, and risin' wi' the lark ;
The denties then were tatties and oatmeal—
We lived on them, and aye thrived unco weel.
But Providence was sair against us then,
We left oor bonnie farmstead in the glen ;
We lost oor brawest cattle wi' the plague,
And faither's year-auld cowt fell ower the craig.
Oor fields o' wheat and rye and yellow grain
Lay drookit, hashed, and rotten in the rain ;
My auldest brither ran awa' to sea,
And I gaed to a farm and took a fee.
It's lang since then, but weel I mind o't yet,

'Twas Providence, and I maun jist submit;
That waefu' e'en I gaed I'll ne'er forget,
The cart wi' faither standin' at the yett,
The sair-begritten wee things gethered roond,
My faither, aye stoot-hearted, fair broke doun;
My mither waved till I was oot o' sicht,
Her kind face whiter in the gloamin' licht:
That face again on earth I never saw—
She died when I was gane, and left us a';
My faither mourned her sair when she was dead,
Folk said he never lifted up his head.
Fu' cheerily he bore his ills till then,
And said " What has been broken we can mend;"
But mither's death was mair than he could bide—
He dwined awa', and noo lies by her side.
Ay, Jamie, lad, aye mind, whate'er betide,
To mak' kind Providence yer help and guide.
" Was't Providence that wasted a' the rye, Jamie,
That fell't the year-auld cowt, and killed the kye,
That made yer auldest brither gang to sea,
And sent ye till a farm to tak' a fee?
Was't that set my faither's stooks on fire,
And blew the sparks aboot and burnt the byre?"
Hech! laddie, stop, for guidsake say nae mair.
My crasie cap's clean lifted frae my hair;
Blame Providence for what we dae oorsel'!
Na! Jamie, laddie, na, that winna tell.
Oor Rabbie says that " Man was made to mourn"—
Sma' comfort that to hearts wi' sorrow torn;
Puir sinfu' man is aye his ain warst friend,

But Providence throws gowden glints atween
The ills that sin has brocht upon us a';
But e'en when ithers' ills upon us fa',
They work together for oor lastin' guid.
Like clouds that gether till the sun is hid,
Then break in blessin' on ilk' flower and tree,
Sae e'en deals Providence wi' you and me.
Tho' aiblins a' we dinna understand,
Aye learn in a' things here to trace His hand;
Nae scholar's lore hae I, but common sense
Has taught me aye to trust in Providence;
I ken my clouds hae a' been silver-lined,
And, oh ! I ken that Providence is kind.

## BRING THEM HOME.

HAVE you wealth of wishes kind ?
      Bring them home.
Manners cheerful and refined ?
      Bring them home.
Are you loved by all around ?
Are your words in laughter drowned ?
Let the dear home-walls resound—
      Bring them home.

Have you pleasant words to say ?
      Bring them home.
Have you compliments to pay ?
      Bring them home.
Songs of sympathy or mirth ?
Let them echo round the hearth—
'Tis the dearest spot on earth—
      Bring them home.

Have you sorrows none can share ?
      Bring them home.
Would you ease the griefs you bear ?
      Bring them home.
Come where gloomy cares take flight,.
In the lustre of its light,
Here all eyes are sparkling bright—
      Bring them home.

Have you friends you long to know?
　　　Bring them home.
Bring them to the warm hearth's glow—
　　　Bring them home.
Bid each welcome as a guest
Of the hearts who love you best;
Would you put them to the test ?
　　　Bring them home.

Have you precious gems of truth?
　　　Bring them home.
Let them crown the brow of youth—
　　　Bring them home.
While the voice of wisdom calls,
And the light of glory falls
On the everlasting walls—-
　　　Bring them home.

## A THANKFUL HEART.

I NEED it more than gems or gold,
Than luxuries which wealth unfold,
This treasure which is never old—
  A thankful heart.

Than honours fame may here bequeath ;
Than sceptre, crown, or laurel wreath ;
Their estimate is far beneath
  A thankful heart ;

Than pleasure in variety,
In what is termed society ;
Than freezing forms of piety—
  A thankful heart.

What genial lustre lights the eye,
Reflecting earth, or sea, or sky ;
Each seems so fair when mirrored by
  A thankful heart.

The countless cares that grieve us here
Like shadows flit and disappear ;
How small they seem, for Heaven is near
  A thankful heart.

Then more than wealth, oh ! give it me !
From discontent and envy free,
What angel eyes delight to see—
  A thankful heart.

For every gift kind heaven supplies,
For health and joy let songs arise ;
Be ever shining in our eyes
  A thankful heart.

# THE ANVIL SONG.

THREE jolly smiths are we, my boys,
  We sing the whole day long,
Our hammers make a merry noise
  Upon the anvil strong.
Their measured beat is music sweet,
  The bellows fires our zeal,
We're strong as ore, and to the core
  Our hearts are true as steel.

*Chorus*—Bang, bang, bang, now the anvil's sounding,
  Bang, bang, bang, while the sparks are bounding,
  Merrily, merrily all day long,
  Listen to the anvil song.

And while we bravely strike for gold
  With iron strength and might,
We strike for home like warriors bold,
  For honour, truth, and right.
Would every blow laid falsehood low,
  And raised the truly wise ;
Thus, 'mid the din, our thoughts within
  Like burning sparks arise.

*Chorus*—Bang, bang, bang, now the anvil's sounding,
  Bang, bang, bang, while the sparks are bounding,
  Merrily, merrily all day long,
  Listen to the anvil song.

We envy not the crowns of Kings,
　Nor misers' hoarded spoil ;
We love the joy that labour brings
　The sons of honest toil—
The joys that thrill to temper ill
　When daily toil is o'er ;
And loved ones wait at the cottage gate
　To welcome us once more.

*Chorus*—Bang, bang, bang, now the anvil's sounding,
　Bang, bang, bang, while the sparks are bounding,
　Merrily, merrily all day long,
　Listen to the anvil song.

## "FAITHER'S COMIN' IN."

Six has chappit in the toon,
    Lassie ! redd the flaer ;
Rise, man, Tam, ye feckless loon !
    Quat yer faither's chair !
Rin and meet him, bairnies, rin,
    Haste and bring him ben,
Mak' him happy as a king
    At his ain fire-en'.

        Six has chappit i' the toon,
        Faither's comin' in,
        Redd the house an' set the tea,
        Bring yer faither's shoon ;
        Winter nichts are bleerie, Jean,
        Days are dark'nin' sune,
        Keep the ingle cheerie, lass,
        Faither's comin' in.

Aft I've watched for him at e'en
    In the lang-gaen days ;
Waunert 'mong the brackens green,
    Sauntert on the braes ;
Haste ye ! bring me ben my gown,
    I maun smooth my hair ;
Then I liket faither weel,
    Noo a hantel mair.

        Six has chappit, &c.

Time brings change and trouble, Jean,
   We hae had oor share ;
Kindly cheer and lauchin' een
   Lift the load o' care.
Laddies, ye are growin' fast ;
   Though ye a' were men,
Mind ye, faither maun be king
   At his ain fire-en'.

      Six has chappit i' the toon,
      Faither's comin' in,
      Redd the hoose an' set the tea,
      Bring yer faither's shoon ;
      Winter nichts are bleerie, Jean,
      Days are dark'nin' sune,
      Keep the ingle cheerie, lass,
      Faither's comin' in.

## THE SERMON ON THE MOUNT.

A PREACHER preached a sermon gran'
    Awa' in Palestine,
And siccan a fine discourse to man
    Has never been heard sin' syne.

Upon a grassy knowe He stood,
    Far up aboon the steer;
And some had come to laugh at guid,
    And ithers had come to hear.

The gran' auld toon lay weel in view,
    Life's tide at ebb-an'-flow;
He lookèd aboon to the bonnie blue,
    Then doon on the croods below.

The puir man, wi' his hard-earned pey,
    Gaun hame to his ain fire-en',
Was josselt sair tae clear the wey
    For selfish and sinfu' men.

He peetied the men, wi' kindly tear,
    Who had grown rich in sin;
And He said, " The puir man's best aff here,
    For his is the Kingdom aboon."

He saw the mourners wi' a bier
　Gaun by aneath the hill ;
Quo' He, " They're blest that greet doon here,
　For they shune will laugh their fill."


And a' for guid wha hunger sair,
　And search wi' might and main,
O' righteousness they'll get their share
　When mysteries are made plain.


And bless the canny, kindly chiel'
　Ye hardly hear ava ;
His name's respeckit, and atweel
　He has a' folk at his ca'.


An' no the least amang them a',
　Bless the mercifu' ! quo' He ;
They'll never want in My Father's ha'
　Wha hae aye sae much tae gie.


Aboon the lave by Heaven blest,
　The pure in heart hae grace ;
They aiblins ken My Faither best,
　For they see Him face to face.


And they wha dinna bicker here,
　But rin the strife tae quell,
My Faither ca's them bairnies dear—
　They're the likest tae Himsel'.

Be brisk an' cantie a' ye guid
    When sinfu' men misca' ;
Your walth frae spitefu' e'en is hid,
    And ye're clean aboon them a'.


The crood has gaen, the nicht fa's near,
    The Lord is left His lane —
The King of Glory hadna here
    A hoose tae ca' His ain.


And while adoon the hillocks green
    The folk were gaun their wey,
Some said, wi' tear-draps in their een,
    " O ! I could hear Him aye !"


Some peetied Him wha peetied a',
    And kent na' sin nor shame,
While the Preacher's thoughts were far awa'
    In a neuk o' His ain braw hame.

# TO JEANIE.

WHAT's the matter now, my Queenie ?
  Bonnie eyes are full of tears ;
Do they call you "little" Jeanie,
  And you'll soon be seven years ?

There are tall flowers in the meadow,
  Tiny violets, shy and meek ;
Both are nightly gemmed with dew-drops,
  Like the tears upon your cheek.

And the Hand that decks the lily
  Ne'er forgets the fairybell,
Hiding 'neath the fern and bracken,
  Waving o'er the mountain fell.

Little sister, quiet your fears,
  Rosy cheeks has little Jane ;
Do not spoil these eyes with tears,
  Though petite, you might be vain.

Do you know the flower that's fairest
  Hides its head 'mong mossy green ?
Do you know the gem that's rarest
  Is but by its sparkle seen ?

P

# THE AULD-STANE BRAE.

Gang westward 'mang the heather broon
　　As far as ye can win,
There stan's a wee auld-fashioned toon,
　　'Mang thistles, broom, and whin.
Oh! weel I mind o't when a bairn,
　　Hoo oft at gloamin' grey
I've scampered wi' my playmates
　　Down the auld-stane brae.

The cheerie toon, the bonnie toon,
　　Whaur first I saw the morn ;
Wi' hoosies jummelt up and doon
　　'Neath rowan shade and thorn.
'Mang whinnie knowes, whaur Calder rows,
　　I winna hae them say
I hinna sung the praises
　　O' the auld-stane brae.

In dreams I see the blinburn fa'
　　In foam-flakes owre the fell ;
And in the village far awa'
　　I hear the auld wark bell.
Ilk' bairnie kens her daddy weel,
　　Though black as ony slae ;
An' runs fu' blythe to meet him
　　On the auld-stane brae.

My mither aye wi' couthie care,
   As only mithers can,
Toshed up the ribands in oor hair
   As off to school we ran.
" Noo tak' yer school-books and be gaun,"
   I've often heard her say ;
"Tak' hands and gang thegither
   Up the auld-stane brae."

And here are flowers o' mony a tint,
   And hills wi' heath aflame,
Here welcome shines wi' cheerie glint .
   Frae mony a happy hame.
On fields and streams, like sunny beams,
   Sic tender memories play;
Love sheds a bonnie glimmer
   Ower the auld-stane brae.

## THE EVERLASTING ARMS.

ARE you tired, my sisters and brothers ?
Are you weary and sick of the fight ?
As the tired children go to their mothers,
Are you coming to Jesus to-night ?
He will soothe you and hush you to slumber,
And the sound of His voice—how it charms !
From the world's unrest,
Come and lean upon His breast,
And be safe in "the everlasting arms."

> *Refrain*—The Eternal God is thy refuge,
>                 Though life is a sea of alarms,
>                 And the rough winds that blow
>                 Only rock me to and fro—
>                 Safe in "the everlasting arms."

Safe and close to His heart he has bound us,
He knows we are weak and so frail ;
Everlasting the arms that are around us,
And nought 'gainst their power can prevail.
Now His calm voice the tempest is stilling,
And the dream with its dread never harms :
Calm and sweet we will sleep,
Though the billows rise and leap,
Safe in "the everlasting arms."

> *Refrain*—The Eternal God is thy refuge,
>                 Though life is a sea of alarms,
>                 And the rough winds that blow
>                 Only rock me to and fro—
>                 Safe in "the everlasting arms."

## A LITTLE WHILE.

A LITTLE while in life's fresh morn we wake,
Pure as the lilies opening by the lake,
And morning pleasures on our visions break—
    Only a little while.

A little while to romp the lawn at play,
To learn our little tasks at close of day,
To clasp our hands while mother hears us pray—
    Only a little while.

A little while with wonder-beaming eyes,
To view the budding earth, the sea, the skies ;
To wake the echo of a thousand "whys,"
    Only a little while.

A little while the dreams of youth inspire,
We sound the deeper notes of life's grand lyre,
While sets the sun upon a sea of fire—
    Only a little while.

A little while, and oh, so much to do !
The harvest great, the labourers so few,
Amid the shadow-life to grasp the true—
    Only a little while.

A little while, the strife will not be long,
To cheer the sorrowful and right their wrong ;
To watch, to wait, to suffer, and grow strong—
    Only a little while.

# THE POET.

You ask the poet why he sings,
And thus he answers thee—
" Ask Nature why the brooklet flows,
And why the summer blossom grows,
And why the dew-drops gem the rose,
And why the petals ope and close,
And birdies sing in spring,
And why they mount the azure sky ?"
For if they tell the reason why,
He'll tell you why he sings.

You ask the poet why he sings,
When none will list his song ?
The hawthorn, by the dusty road,
Unsought, its fragrance sheds abroad ;
Some beauteous flower gems the sod
Where human foot has never trod,
Unsung, unsought it springs.
Go ! ask of it the reason why ;
Perchance 'twill ope its golden eye
And tell you why he sings.

Oh, world, the poet loves to sing,
Thou canst not hush his song ;

In spite of thee the floweret grows,
The skylark sings, the brooklet flows,
The oft-neglected buds unclose ;
And back the scoffer's scorn he throws,
For hark, the angels whisper nigh,
He tunes his lyre with raptured sigh,
To God his sweetest strains belong,
Who dowered him with the gift of song.

## "T E A R S."

Weep ! weep !
Heart, art thou motionless ?
Is not thy fount of woe
Charged now to overflow ?
Stagnant, devotionless ;
      Sorrowing deep,
Would thou could'st weep !

Tears, tears,
Quenching the fever heat,
Brilliant and diamond spray,
Washing the blight away,
Sweetest and bitterest ;
      Quelling the fears,
Heart-healing tears.

Weep, weep,
Smiles can't deceive us now,
Sad lights revealing all ;
Let the dew freshening fall,
Soothing the burning brow ;
      Grief cannot sleep,
Heavy eyes weep !

Tears, tears,
Passionate bitter showers ;
Earth to her sorrowing
Gives, without borrowing
Dark wintry hours,
      Death wounds and jeers,
God gives us tears.

# "AN ALLEGORY."

I sought thee a gift, sweet baby Grace,
    For the morning of thy birth ;
And I searched for a space the most beautiful place
    I could find in this wonderful earth.

But everything there, though charmingly fair,
    Was but passing as a dream ;
And never a sound broke the silence around
    But the song of a shallow stream.

And I saw a fairy, so mystic and airy,
    In her flowery bower stand ;
Her robes were bright as the starry light
    She held within her hand.

Blue were her eyes, as the bright summer skies,
    But cold as the light of morn ;
Her gleaming hair like the sunset fair
    O'er a field of ripened corn.

She said, Was it flowers from my sunny bowers
    Bade thee seek this beauteous glen ?
Would'st thou have the fate of the honoured and great ?
    Come ! pluck from each yielding stem.

I seek a gift for a child, I said,
　Who must travel a toilsome way ;
Alone she must climb from the vale of time
　To the heights of eternal day.


Full well I believe that their charms deceive—
　For e'en now I can espy,
Low lurking 'neath the verdant leaf,
　The serpent's glittering eye.


Lo ! now I ween, saith the fairy Queen,
　That thy jealous fear is vain.
Why ! wilt thou scorn for life's fair morn
　The flowery path of fame ?


But take this wreath for the dear young head,
　Or, perchance, this ring will please ;
But I turned from the gaudy toys, and said—
　Fair Queen ! not these ! not these !


I've heard wild storms o'er the mountains rise ;
　And the golden ring will rust,
And the pearl, the gem, and the diadem
　Will dwindle into dust.


Oh ! linger still, the bright fairy sighed,
　I'll give her beauty and grace ;
But Grace is her name, fair Queen, I cried,
　And beauty lights her face.

I must bid farewell to thy witching dell
   And thy sweetly-scented bower ;
For beautiful things will soon take wings,
   And wither in an hour.


Swift vengeance follow on thy path !
   Then did the fairy cry ;
For whoso dares a fairy's wrath
   Must also dare to die.


Dost thou indeed my gifts deride,
   And scorn my magic power ?
And trample on my queenly pride
   Within my regal bower ?


Go now ! pursue thy wilful way ;
   But where thy feet shall tread,
The sun, with fierce relentless ray,
   Shall scorch thy haughty head.


But, heedless of her wrath, I sang
   Along the pleasant way :
Thy words are vain, as is thy name,
   Thou Queen of Vanity.


But soon, by that dread fairy cursed,
   The path grew wild and bare,
And through the clouds the red sun burst
   With fierce and angry glare.

Nor could I find a cooling shade
From his fierce wrath to fly,
For every tree within that glade
Did fade, and droop, and die.

And everywhere his reddening glare
My aching thirst did mock ;
But, looking round, I shelter found
Beneath a mighty rock.

And flowing from its riven side
I saw, as in a dream,
Far roll in circling eddies wide
A pure refreshing stream.

And as I stood in doubt to think
Whence all this flood might be,
I heard a loving voice say, " Drink,
This rock was cleft for thee."

And gaily, lo ! above, below,
The wood with echoes rang ;
The foliage shook, fast fled the brook
The bracken groves among.

And, lo ! I saw with sore affright
A traveller from afar ;
I could not brook his eye so bright—
'Twas like the morning star :

He showed me straight the path to heaven,
    And he bade me not despair.
" Behold !" saith he, " what the King hath given
    The little one to wear."

And he gave to me a helmet strong,
    A shining burnished shield,
A breastplate clear, when the foe is near,
    A sword for the battlefield ;

A mystic glass through which to view,
    The happy land afar,
When storms rage loud, and the thunder-cloud
    Hides the light of sun or star.

This glorious crown, when arms are laid down,
    And the long, long journey done,
I'll keep, saith he, till victory
    By the soldier shall be won.

I wept, when he faded from my sight,
    Waving a last adieu ;
I the armour bright took with delight,
    And I hastened to bring it you.

## "THE TOOM FIRE-EN'.'

"Oh! Maggie, heard ye ever sic a din?
I think ye'll maist be frichtit tae come in :
But come in-owre, an' rest yersel' a wee,
I've jist put on the kettle for oor tea.
Oh ! sic a hoose, ye'll hardly fin' a chair,
Ye'll think they're dancin' reels across the flair ;
My certy, Maggie, I've my ain adae,
Wi' richt hard wark I ne'er hae time to play.
Thae bairns are gabblin' like as mony geese ;
Bob ! div' ye hear me, will ye haud yer peace ?
His dragon's tail is fankled roond his feet,
Gae, lowse him, Kate, an' let him to the street ;
Wull, fin' anither place to stott yer ba',
Ye'll smash doon a' the dishes frae the wa'.
I think there ne'er wis woman tried like me—
Be aff an' gie us quaiteness for a wee ;
That dirty flair hae I this day scoured weel,
Redd up my grate, an' polished a' the steel ;
I cleaned thae bairns, and look hoo they've come hame ;
Their een, the brats—they canna blacken them—
Keek oot o' faces smeart wi' stour an' mud,
Like specks o' blue oot-owre a thunder-clud.
This couthie wee thing slaisters a' my goun,
Syne raxes to my hair and glaums it doon.
The guidman never sees me oot the bit,
When at the warst, I'm shure tae hear his fit,

But John's a man I never heard complain ;
Wi' cheerie face he tak's the skirlin' wean,
I run tae set the table for his tea,
Half-donnert, like a body on the spree.
Oh ! Maggie, hoo I envy ye at e'en,
Your weel-toshed hoose, wi' a' things trig and bein ;
Your glancin' grate glints back the ingle lowe,
Your braw geraniums (mine'll never grow)
Haud up their heids against the window peen,
Their bonnie blossoms glintin' through the green ;
Your tabby purrs—the hearth is a' her ain—
Oor cat, sair tousel't, worn tae skin and bane,
Like hunted creatur', skelps across the flair,
And keeps her guard aneath the guidman's chair ;
Your Tam comes hame tae fin' ye trig an' braw,
Your hair aye snod, and apron like the snaw,
Your kettle singin' and your teapot het,
Your hoose aye shinin', and your table set.
Hoo strangely things are ordered here, the taen
Has far ower muckle wark, the tither nane.
Losh ! Maggie, hae I vex'd ye ?  Tak' your tea,
I'm shure ye needna heed the like o' me."

Quo' Maggie—" Whaur's the heart that's free frae care ?
Noo hear me, Jean, an' envy me nae mair
O' my toom house, and heart that's jist as toom,
When your cup's fu' and rinnin' owre the brim ;
Ye kent na, Jean, that mine was ance as fu'.
There was a time I channert sair like you,
Oor wark ahin', and weans aye in my road ;

And noo I've laid them a' aneath the sod.
Aye, Jeanie, greet yer fill, I canna greet.
What wad I gie to hear my bairnies' feet ?
I wish my flair was marked frae en' to en'
Wi' wee feet rinnin' but and toddlin' ben ;
I wish their toys aboot my hearth were spread,
Though ance, like you, I thocht I'd like it redd.
It's redd noo, Jeanie, and I'm left alane ;
The hoose is redd, but, oh ! the bairns are gane ;
Nane seekin' pieces fash me ony mair,
Nae bairnies cress my goun or pu' my hair."

Quo' Jean—" Forgie me, I'm a sinfu' woman ;
Oh ! Maggie, should sic days for me be comin',
What wad life be if we were left alane ?
E'en if the weest o' them a' were taen,
Or Bob or Wull or Kate, oh, God, forgie me !
And though I've grummelt lang aye leaves them wi' me.
Aye, Maggie, your wee lambs are a' at rest,
Wi' Ane aboon, who lo'es them far the best ;
But, woman, what you've said I'll ne'er forget,
As lang's I leeve I'll bless the day we met.
And, oh ! may He who gies us a' we hae,
Whose arm uphauds us in the partin' day,
Lang keep us free frae skaith and trouble sair,
And leave us aye oor bairns—we'll ne'er be puir.

# FAREWELL.

'Tis sad to bid a last adieu
To friends whose love is tried and true,
Though 'twere but for a little while,
To miss the bright familiar smile,
And know not when or where we'll clasp
That hand in friendship's loving grasp.

Deep mystery holds the golden spell,
And who the when or where may tell?
Whether on earth or heaven above,
God knoweth—yea! and God is Love.
His promise sure brings comfort sweet;
Though sundered here, we all shall meet.

Oh! may His presence shield and guide,
When tossed upon the heaving tide,
And wing thee safe with eagle flight
O'er wildest waves in darkest night.
Rejoice! thy Pilot wise is He
Who stilled the storm on Galilee.

And when between us far and wide
Old ocean rolls with ceaseless pride,
Have still for us a gentle thought;
When far away forget us not,
Who when we kneel at evening prayer
Commend thee to our Father's care.

Q

We yet may clasp your hand once more
On much-loved Scotia's rugged shore ;
Or where the vines grow rich and high,
'Neath brighter sun and bluer sky,
Where strange flowers spring in sunny glades,
And bright birds thrill the forest shades ;

Or far, where tower 'neath golden skies,
The mansions of loved paradise,
Where tears of suffering never flow,
Nor partings rend the heart with woe ;
By pearly gate or golden street,
Though sundered far, we all shall meet.

# THE UNANSWERED PRAYER.

A WISH to God in secret I expressed,
For prayer was ever found the golden key
To the great depths of Love's unfathomed sea,
And, nothing doubting, waited to be blest.

Our Father bending, read my upward glance
As earthly fathers read, and realize
Unspoken thoughts that light their children's eyes—
Hopes unconfined as heaven's blue expanse.

And lo! an angel from His presence passed,
With wings down-drooping slowly to my side;
While I expectant spied, He could not hide
That *No!* cold, chilling, cruel as the blast.

My trembling heart had God's approval deep,
While lowly supplicating at the throne;
Methought that No! would turn my heart to stone,
Oh! for refreshing tears, sweet tears to weep!

Father! Thy flowers in sunshine blossom high,
Deep violets and roses red and white;
Dost Thou withhold them sunshine, rain, and light?
Then muse in silent wonder that they die,

Even as the flower, this hope had birth from Thee,
Awoke to prayer, by Thy spirit fanned ;
O'er blight and blast and suffering, to expand
High as the heaven, unfettered as the sea.

Thine answer now more clearly I define,
Which cost Thee more to speak than me to hear ;
Thy heart throbs ache for ache and tear for tear,
My cares, my joys, and sorrows all are Thine.

Since then the Master I have loved and served,
In watchings oft and perils lone and late,
For higher good the answer is reserved,
And for the blessing I serenely wait.

Yet shalt thou bring me back mine olive spray,
Forth o'er the deep I send thee, wandering dove ;
Yet shall I see the gloom dissolve in love,
And hear the angel whisper, " It is Yea !"

# TOGETHER.

TOGETHER in the long ago
   We roamed the rural scene,
I heard thee call, and followed slow
O'er stones which stemmed the current's flow,
   'Twixt bracken banks of green.
I hear thee still, yet cannot go ;
   For Jordan rolls between.

Together, time, how brief it seems,
   Since last we romped and played ;
The sun shot fiery golden gleams
Through bending shades beside the streams,
   In autumn leaves arrayed :
But memory calls from flitting dreams
   My thoughts, that far have strayed.

Together in the glad old years,
   I followed stone by stone,
But now mine eyes are dim with tears,
And through their mist thy form appears,
   I call thee, thou art gone ;
Thy voice is ringing in mine ears,
   But I must walk alone.

Alone I stand, yet not alone,
   Beneath the dusky pine,
Though streams be dark, with moss o'ergrown,
O'er moorland marsh, in paths unknown,
   One human, yet divine,
Will lead me safe from stone to stone,
   And clasp your hand in mine.

# IMMORTALITY.

THE waves are dying on the shore,
　The day is dying in the west,
　In golden leaves the groves are dressed ;
Yet thou, my soul, hast much in store,
　For thou shalt never die.


Though Nature hastens to decay,
　And every leaf and flower fade ;
　And 'neath the vernal turf is laid
Thy earthly tenement of clay,
　Yet thou shalt never die.


Though lightnings flash and thunders roll,
　And earth's foundations shrink and shake,
　And hills and mountains melt and quake,
And heaven falls like a flaming scroll,
　Yet thou shalt never die.


When yonder sun will light no more,
　And moon and stars have passed away,
　And countless years seem but a day,
Soar, thou celestial spirit, soar,
　For thou shalt never die.

Through mists of doubt and dashing spray,
  Choose well thy pilot ere he steers
  Full in the light of endless years ;
Where shalt thou spend eternity ?
  For thou shalt never die.

## CHRISTMASTIDE.

(May be sung to the music of Schubert's "Ave Maria.")

SOFT the moonbeams stealing down
  Glimmer on the pearly snow ;
Winter dons his dazzling crown,
  Icy gems all quaintly glow.
Joy ! the Prince of Peace is born,
  Fears are vanquished, hopes arise ;
Pure as blossom on the thorn
  Low in Bethlehem's stall He lies—
            Give Him the glory !

Give Him glory ! crown Him King !
  Joyously in chorus break ;
Angels bright on snowy wing
  Through the stars their journey take.
Peace on earth, they sing again,
  How the ringing music swells ;
Hearty, right goodwill to men !
  Ring the grand old Christmas bells !
            Give Him the glory !

Give Him glory ! crown Him now !
  Loyally His life He gave ;
Gems of beauty for His brow
  Are the souls He died to save.
Earth puts on her bridal robe,
  Night displays her jewelled tyre ;
Round the cycle of the globe,
  Fly, oh ! Love, on wings of fire—
            Give Him the glory !

# Personal and Press Opinions of Miss Darling's previous volume, "Poems and Songs."

### PROFESSOR BLACKIE.

They are spiritual songs of rare beauty and fragrance, and well deserve the circulation they have enjoyed. Some of them are as good as the best sermons, and a great deal better than many sermons.

### REV. PRINCIPAL MORISON, D.D.

I have been dipping into your attractive volume, and the more frequently I return to dip again, the more do I like to go. I see in your pieces a genuine vein of poetry.

### REV. PROFESSOR FERGUSON, D.D.

Miss Darling, whose poems have so frequently pleased and delighted the readers of the "Christian News," needs no recommendation from me as to her ability and the worth of her productions. I have perused her former volume with deep interest, finding in it marks of a refined mind and traces of true genius, while the verses are eminently calculated to edify the Christian.

### REV. PRINCIPAL CAIRD, D.D.

Miss Darling's poems, especially the Scottish ones, manifest no little poetic feeling, and are full of tenderness and pathos. In common with all her readers I hope that she may long contribute to their gratification by the renewed exercise of her poetic gifts.

### REV. DAVID MACRAE.

Here we have practical Christianity in her beautiful garment of song. The book is full of warmth and comfort, wisdom, sweet charity, and home affection. One can sit down to it as in front of a cosy fire on a winter's eve.

### A. J. SYMINGTON, F.R.S.N.A.

You have a keen eye for the beauty of the outward world. "Scotia Mountainland" has a glowing fervour and true patriotic ring which will carry it, music-winged, round the globe.

### PRINCIPAL DYER, C.E., M.A., D.Sc.

I value this gift for its intrinsic worth. It contains a great amount of common-sense philosophy and insight into human nature, combined with great poetic power.

### REV. WILLIAM DUNLOP.

Miss Darling's poetry is full of health and good humour, and of that practical wisdom which pertains to domestic felicity.

R

### ANNIE S. SWAN.

That little poem, "My Home," is my favourite. It is perfect poetry. If you never write anything more beautiful or more true you need not fret. And I like "Bring them Home," "Withered Leaves," "The Agnostic," "Triumphs of Thought," and "Faither's comin' in," the Scotch of which is very pure.

### MARY CROSS.

Long may you charm us with thoughts so pure, so lovingly sympathetic, expressed with such grace and sweetness. It is no idle flattery to say that Scotland, as well as England, will have her Hemans.

### LADY DILKE.

In looking over your pages I have been especially pleased with the "Bairnie," the gay humour of which, melting into a touch of serious pathos at the close, is very happily expressed.

### EDWARDS' "MODERN SCOTTISH POETS."

Miss Darling is a thoughtful and gifted poetess. In her poems we find many apt utterances and felicitous ideas in really artistic setting, and never miss the mysterious something known as the spirit of true poetry. Her sympathies are warm and broad. She pleads for all who are out in the cold, through bodily or spiritual need, and it is in such utterances as hers that one detects the glad faith that transforms life's thorns into roses.

### PEOPLE'S FRIEND, DUNDEE.

This dainty little volume should be in every home. There is music in every line Miss Darling writes, and the best evidence of this is the number of her pieces set to music in our pages. "Scotia Mountainland" is a song which for patriotic fire and sentiment it will be difficult to surpass. Miss Darling speaks directly to the heart through the medium of the domestic affections. Take as delightful examples, "Mother," "Faither's comin' in," "The Toom Fire-en'," "The Sisters' Strife," and "The wee Lost Laddie." As a poetic gem, which we do not think is surpassed in the English language, we name "The Motherless Babe." We heartily recommend the book to our readers, to whom the Author is well and lovingly known.

### SCOTTISH LEADER, EDINBURGH.

We have not detected one faulty line in all the 240 pages. Songs of home and the affections—short didactic and religious poems—have all a simplicity and directness of expression, and a breezy haleness and purity of tone which make them very pleasant reading.

### SALTCOATS AND ARDROSSAN HERALD.

The Author's teachings as a poetess are of the right sort. Her reflective subjects are treated in an earnest, direct way, and full

( 3 )

of practical common-sense. "The Toom Fire-en'" is a powerful
poem, written in terse doric, full of human nature and deep
pathos, touching and true. In "Life Echoes" how lightly she
touches the lyre, yet how far-reaching is its music. "The
Anvil Song" has a ring of the charming songs of labour by
Carmen Sylva. The last verse from the poem "Words" should
be written in letters of gold.

**PEOPLE'S JOURNAL, DUNDEE.**

Her fancy ranges over a wide field, and she touches no theme
which she does not adorn. To all that she writes she imparts a
deep moral and religious tone which renders her poems at once
pleasing and instructive.

**WEEKLY CITIZEN, GLASGOW.**
("ORION.")

"Poems and Songs" is a volume of graceful verse. Miss
Darling is particularly happy in dealing with children or child
life. Take, for example, "The Boys are Away," or the capital
verses on the "Boy and a Penny."

**MONTROSE STANDARD.**

A sweet and interesting collection of poetical pieces in a great
variety of measures, and on many different themes, well fitted to
please and profit.

**HAMILTON ADVERTISER.**

Genius seems determined to adorn the bleak parish of Shotts
with a halo of poetic glory. Isabella F. Darling is a native of
Shotts, and a true singer. Her poems flow freely and naturally as
a mountain stream; rare originality of conception, pervaded
with a tender sacred impressiveness. Always ennobling, it is
sure to be welcomed by all lovers of genuine poetry.

**WISHAW PRESS.**

Since Janet Hamilton has passed away her mantle seems to
have fallen on Isabella F. Darling. What strikes us most
forcibly in her writings is the high-toned patriotism that inspires
her songs. Miss Darling has invested the Scottish "Fire-en'"
with a romance and dignity of its own. "The Agnostic" is a
spirited attack on the school of Herbert Spencer, and an exposure
of the inherent weakness of its negative creed. "Poems and
Songs" may be compared to the picturesque and sunny braes of
her native Lanarkshire.

**CLYDESIDE LITTERATEURS.**

In every production of her pen she strikes a high key,
inculcating a moral lesson which, though never obtrusive, is
dwelt on in no halting measure. As proof of her exceptional
ability to compose songs, we have only to refer to "Scotia
Mountain Land" or "The Laddie I Lo'e." There is a rugged
vigour in the former which stirs the blood and awakens patriotic
fire.

### LARGS AND MILLPORT NEWS.

The longest poem in the book, entitled "A Certain Rich Man," is treated with no little dramatic force and skill, and tenderly and loyally has she sung of the scenes that cluster round the home and hearth.

### SCOTTISH NIGHTS.

The musical expression of pure thought and fine feeling. Pleasant reading in a pleasant form.

### CHRISTIAN NEWS.

Her poems have the ring of true poetic fervour and genius.

### THE FIRESIDE PICTORIAL MAGAZINE.

There is considerable variety in the subjects of which she treats, and her sympathies are warm and broad. The fine poem entitled " She hath done what she could," speaks for itself.

### MOTHERWELL TIMES.

From the perusal of it we are sure our readers will rise feeling better, encouraged, and cheered. The poems deal mostly with life in its various phases, with here and there a touch of nature, a fresh whiff from the country, showing that the author is keenly alive to its influences, and has the true poetic insight and quick eye for the beauties of mountain and glen. She also touches with sympathic hand the pathetic side of life.

### STIRLING JOURNAL AND ADVERTISER.

She writes on many themes, on home and the home circle. There are also didactic and religious poems, all characterised by truth, sweetness, and purity of tone. Her liltings are like the low sweet song of the robin heard when autumn leaves fall thickly, and October blasts warn us that wintry days are near. The volume is handsomely got up.

### GLASGOW CITIZEN.

Miss Darling's rhythm is easy and unconstrained. Some of the poems and songs manifest a distinct sense of humour.

### BRECHIN ADVERTISER.

Miss Darling possesses true poetic genius, and her gift has been wisely used. She does not appeal merely to the intellect, but her reflections are calculated to reach the inner citadel of the heart. Her genuine moral earnestness finds ready expression when dealing with social scenes and phases of life around her. While some of her sweet and musical lilts are far-reaching and tender, others are strong, stirring, and patriotic. Indeed, there is much of the ideal of true poetry throughout this volume.

### WEEKLY NEWS, DUNDEE.

A healthy, fresh, and elevating sweetness pervades the writings of this author, also a lively sense of humour.

www.ingramcontent.com/pod-product-compliance
Lightning Source LLC
Chambersburg PA
CBHW030816020726
47499CB00006B/1936